W9-DGR-852

DEADLY NIGHTSHADE

By the same author

As James Fraser

THE EVERGREEN DEATH

A COCK-PIT OF ROSES

As Alan White

DEATH FINDS THE DAY

THE WHEEL

THE LONG NIGHT'S WALK

THE LONG DROP

JAMES FRASER

DEADLY NIGHTSHADE

HARCOURT, BRACE & WORLD, INC.
NEW YORK

First American edition

ISBN 0-15-124065-5

Library of Congress Catalog Card Number: 71-124823

Printed in the United States of America

For
Mr and Mrs Wood
with thanks

J. F.

CHAPTER ONE

Mrs Gibbins was an artist. The subject of her paintings, she said, was dictated to her by God, a 'manifestation' guided her brush strokes, and she mixed the colours herself, though she didn't deny a certain Satanic intervention in her frequent use of scarlet lake, even for features. All the canvases left in Bent Hall when Jeremy Bent emigrated had been overpainted many times, and beneath her impasto were rumoured to be three Constables, a Joshua Reynolds, and several Brueghels. Since Mrs Gibbins felt that canvas size was a limitation, her artistic efforts from time to time lapped in full stream over the walls and ceilings of all the principal rooms of the Hall.

Joe Verney, the Bent constable, was one of few privileged to see this art collection in its entirety; patrolling the grounds of the Hall was his nightly responsibility and very occasionally, Mrs Gibbins asked him inside.

One evening, so he reports, he heard terrible groaning from the opened window of a cloakroom abutting the timbered dining hall. When he drew nearer, suddenly he heard the voice of Mrs Gibbins pleading, it seemed, to the Heavens above. "Dear Lord," she called, "vouchsafe me this day, here and now, forsaking all others, that I may be granted a motion."

Whereupon, the constable said later in the pub with a wicked and irreverent turn of phrase, presumably the Spirit moved her! Constable Joe Verney chuckled as he remembered this incident, late one night, patrolling the grounds of Bent Hall. He'd made his 'point' on the Green by the War Memorial. Grove Gardens next, in the front gate of Bent Hall, up the main drive with the copse on his left hand, the pond back on his right. Bent Hall was ahead, top of the drive, main house across in front of him, dining room and galleries in the wing stretching back on the left, orangery back on the right. Beyond the orangery were the rose gardens, facing east. Daft place to put a rose garden, ought to be facing south by rights. Which way round? Some nights he went clockwise, others anti. Anti tonight. Along the front of the house, no sign of life, round the orangery, and what the hell's that in the rose garden? A dog? Brian King's labrador by the looks of it. "Here, Falstaff, good dog!" he called. Falstaff came dashing with that wobbling hip movement typical of the breed.

"Tha' shouldn't be in here, Falstaff," Joe said. The dog pressed its snout under his hand hoping for a caress. Dogs get like that if they're brought into the house, stroked and fed biscuits, Joe thought. Nothing worse than a ruined Labrador. He fondled its muzzle a couple of times in pity, then set off, quietly calling 'heel'. The dog hadn't been properly trained, of course, and didn't know where 'heel' was. It kept darting, backwards and forwards, side to side, snuffling in the grass, sniffing tree trunks. "Come here, you silly sod," Joe called and settled it behind him. Falstaff seemed to realise something of Joe's frustration; he trotted more or less at his heel round the back of the orangery, along the stables behind the Hall, the wash houses, the store rooms and granary, to the northwest corner. One quick look southwards, down the west side of the Hall. Nothing doing, nothing stirs; a lot of lead down there, gutter pipes, drain boxes emblazoned with the Bent Arms, but so far no-one had had the courage to make the attempt. They will do, one of these nights; one of these Birmingham gangs will find out! But apparently, not tonight! "Not tonight, Falstaff!" Joe said. A dog's a bit of company on a dark night, isn't it? Not that Falstaff'd be much good against a Birmingham gang, running in to get his chin tickled. Joe hated the nightly parade of the Hall grounds. Former glory, gone to rot. Wood once mahogany, brought to powder, straight stone lines that slipped when mortar crumbled, rank growth everywhere. Once proud men walked these paths and gardeners touched a forelock. Maybe one of Verney's ancestors was conceived up there in the servants' quarters as a buxom lass lay under the will of her master. After all, the Master's bedroom connected, by back staircase set behind the fire, to a servants' bedroom two floors above. You never know! Nobility's where you find it, these days! He turned out of the grounds, past the Monkey Puzzle tree that towered a good sixty feet, into Church Row almost opposite the Church, Falstaff behind him. More or less! Bright these June nights, a bit cool but just enough to freshen the atmosphere after a day of muggy sunshine. 'Damn it,' he thought, 'we never get the clean sunshine this far inland. Not like Blackpool or Southend. Sea seems to clean the air somehow, let's the sun come through stronger. Roll on holidays. All these trees don't help, neither!' Turn right by the oak along Church Row, down Bent Hill a peck, left by the poplars back into Church Row continuation, and left at the larches into the police station. Lil would have the cocoa ready; lovely, they were off on holiday tomorrow! The thought sustained him during the last half mile of his beat. When he got in the station he must remember to ring old Brian King, pull his leg about Falstaff chasing sheep. Copse on the left, Tolly's light shines through the trees. Fran and MM have lived there thirty years but still they call it Tolly's, and Tolly's dead these sixty years. Last fifty yards, there's the station my lad, cops among the copse, and when you're through that door your helmet's off for fourteen days. Fourteen days and nights, think of that!

He walked in through the door, dog following.

Damn! The sergeant was sitting there, on the sofa, drinking cocoa. His cocoa, wouldn't be surprised. His mug, anyway!

"Thought I'd drop in, Joe, since you're off tomorrow!"

"Very good of you, sarge, I'm sure!"

"Paper work all done?"

"This early evening."

"Just thought I'd check; we don't want to go away and leave the administration in a muddle, do we?"

Damn it, anybody'd think the sergeant, God forbid, was coming with him.

"Falstaff, what*'ave* you got in your mouth?" Lil asked. Falstaff had made a dash for the fire, was sprawled on the rug, his tail flashing semaphore. Hearing Lil he opened his jaws.

"A bone, is it?" Lil asked, idiotic as women always are with dogs and babies.

"That's a human jaw-bone," the sergeant said, surprisingly calm for such a pronouncement.

"It can't be," Joe wailed, bewildered. "We're going on us 'olidays tomorrow!"

CHAPTER TWO

There must be well over ten thousand trees in Bent, and it's only small as villages go. Sir Beresford Bent, they say, scoured the world looking for specimens, brought 'em back alive from South America and China and planted 'em with loving care. And, of course, a spoonful of rotted horse-muck and roots spread well out but then, Sir Beresford was a methodical man. He bought the land on which Bent was founded on his return from Calcutta and the East India Company that had made his fortune; he built Bent Hall of best Northampton ironstone, fifteen bedrooms and a dining hall famed throughout the Midlands for its timbered ceiling. He filled a conservatory with tropical plants, grew his own oranges and lemons, pineapples and avocado pears, grapes black and white, and seven different varieties of camellia. This was in the early eighteenth century. His first wife gave him an heir and two daughters before she died of the vapours; when he found his second wife in the coach within the coach-house with a groom he thrashed them both to death, remade his will, then ate a handful of the seeds of the Curare tree he'd brought from Brazil whose sap is the deadly poison in which natives dip tips of arrows. Honour first, was the family motto.

Over the years some of the trees died, of course, but many survived by seeding themselves. Now there remains a Travellers' Tree, a Baobab, a Sapodilla, several Ailanthus the Chinese call The Tree of Heaven but which, since the leaves emit a smell of faeces when crushed, is known locally as The Catshit Tree. From seven Camellias only two remain, of the varieties Saluensis and Sasanqua respectively pink and white; each February and May the present gardener George Lines takes up to a thousand blooms and the proceeds from the sale, by tradition, go to The Home for Unmarried Mothers at Birton.

There's no Bent Hall at present. Jeremy Bent gave it to the Nation in 1952 but without adequate endowment; the Nation gave it back. Jeremy, now married to a psychiatric social worker, owns a used car lot in Dayton, Ohio, and has changed his name to Beresford-Bent in view of the Americans' coarser sense of humour. The Beresford-Bents came to England in 1963 to visit the grave of Benjamin Franklin's uncle who used to preach in Bent Church and to show the kids where Pop was born; Mrs Felicia Beresford-Bent, walking up Bent Hill by Scotia's farm, was bitten in the calf by a mongrel dog, and the gross indignity drove them back to Dayton forever.

Only one person now lives in Bent Hall and she's known as Mrs Gibbins in the village though no-one has a clear recollection of her walking up the aisle. She was Miss Gibbins when she turned up in 1942 to keep house for the Comte de Vaspail, who rented Bent Hall from Jeremy's father as a pied-à-terre in England during the war. By the spring of 1943, the Comte had invited forty of his compatriots to live there, an outpost of the Free French Forces. Many agents of the Special Operations Executive, who later dropped into Occupied Europe, were trained there. De Gaulle, it's rumoured, came often during the war, and the word 'merde' can still be seen carved into the trunk of the

Baobab tree; the embroidered lavatory seat covers carry the fleur de lys.

Mrs Gibbins had shut off most of the house, confined herself to a small maid's room by the side door, except during her painting forays. Her window overlooked the front of the house, and she could see clear down the hill to the pond at the bottom.

Unfortunately, she was not looking out of the window when Falstaff found the bone, nor when Joe Verney did his rounds; who knows, if she'd seen them, she might have invited them in and it might have been her carpet on which Falstaff dropped his find.

Friday evening, the night shades were drawn, and Mrs Gibbins painted out her misery.

Friday night in the village, and Lil Verney slowly unpacked two suitcases they were taking to Morecambe. The sergeant had gone with the bone Falstaff found, in a plastic bag bought to keep bacon fresh in the fridge the police house provided. Constable Joe Verney had orders to wait for the bright boys from Birton.

Sam Gainer was in the shop, counting the money; not, as you might expect, to find out how much there was, but to verify he had enough change in the various denominations of coins and notes. Friday night is pay night: Saturday they'd flash fivers, and hell to pay if he couldn't change 'em. Mrs Gainer came into the shop, heavy with a baby. "Cut a slice of ham if you want it for your supper," she said. He reached on the shelf, took a bottle of pickled beetroot and another of Indian Mango chutney. "Spoil me," he said. She kissed him, she was forty and he over fifty, and still they kissed. The new baby did that. "Glad we moved?"

he asked. They'd been living together in another village before they were married. Perversely, when they made it legal, Sam insisted they move. "Let 'em think we've run away to a life of sin together," he said. They'd never been back, never would.

Friday night and reverend dreams of a Holy week-end, a Church swollen with congregation, an inspired sermon. 'God gave this Power of Rhetoric,' he thought, 'the Spoken Word is mightier than the Book.' In Church on Sunday, he'd finally and utterly convince them. Meanwhile, he had the Women's Institute meeting to Think About, and the Parish Council on which he was an Ex-officio Member, and the Youth Club which, though secular, was in his Tender Care, the Arrangements for the Bazaar, and the Old Folk's Concert, the Church Choir outing, and the appointment of a new Verger since old Simon had gone deaf, the question of the central heating for the Church, and he'd heard Nellie Binns had taken bad again and she ought to be Visited, and Shirley Scotia had been asking about confirmation and his own daughter Marina was pregnant again, or so Banley, his wife, said. And her not married! Marina his daughter, that is. Oh dear! No wonder the word was rarely said as powerfully as it might be. Lord grant us Strength, was his prayer. From his pocket he took a copy of *Last Exit to Brooklyn.* Time for a quick read before supper.

Friday night, Fran and Malcolm Minton. Fran and MM as they are known on the joint grocery list are quarrelling again. Well, hardly quarrelling, more having a difference of opinion. Two boiled eggs apiece, bread and butter, salt and pepper, and a cup of coffee each, Fran black, MM with milk. Fran looks at the slices of bread on the side of the plate, between a quarter and three eighths of an inch thick, cut with that sort of precision.

"You do it deliberately," Fran said.

"I've got other things to think about, I can assure you!"

"Sometimes you just try to aggravate me!"

"I never!"

"I've mentioned it over and over again."

"I thought that was what you wanted?"

"You know it isn't. I've been quite specific." It'll go on for half an hour before anyone could realise they're talking about the thickness of the bread, Fran's expressed desire to slim, and MM's conviction that Fran, of whom he is very fond, needs energy. Potatoes on the plate, slivers of fat on the ham, sugar in coffee and milk. Fran would like to give up bread but MM won't allow that.

"One of these days," Fran finally says. "I shall just pack up, and go to my family." The silence you could cut with MM's bread knife. Bother! MM knows he's gone just that bit too far again. It'll take three games of Jotto, and two games of chess, before he'll get Fran round again.

Detective Inspector Bill Aveyard lived in a flat in Birton. Fifteen minutes before he'd pulled the cork on a bottle of Macon bought cheaply at the Co-op supermarket. In the fridge were two steaks cut thick, frozen Brussels sprouts, a tin of new potatoes peeled and ready for the pot. There was a chocolate mousse, and a miniature of Tia Maria he intended to pour over it at the right moment. A long-play Nina Simone was on, the top light was off, leaving the room illuminated only by the standard lamps at each end of the black cirrhus sofa covered with a blanket that passed for a rug in the dim light. On the rug was a wide-eyed young lady. She looked around the room.

"First time you've ever had me here!" she said, in what

he hoped was a prophetic remark. He passed her a gin and tonic.

"I hope it won't be the last," he said. She looked straight into his eyes, holding the glass he'd given her by its stem. Ramon Novarro, Rudolf Valentino, no, too young for that. James Dean who killed himself, Paul McCartney? Get him! Gins and tonic, bottles of wine, black walls, lights out, and a blanket on the sofa. Taking her for granted, wasn't he? Well, why not, girls like it, too.

"That'll depend on you, won't it!"

Something within him took off like an eagle. Zot! Blood really does quicken at moments like that. A small voice whispered, 'You're in luck boy, tonight's the night.'

"Thought'd just let the wine breathe a while before we drink it," he said dead nonchalant! "Then steak, choux de brouxelles, pommes de terre!"

"Quite the gourmet, aren't we?" she said, trying to keep her voice steady. Who wants food? Still, play the game, he's obviously enjoying himself. "And what's for afters?" she asked, innocently.

Telephone. Telephone. Telephone.

It was the Chief Inspector, brief as usual. "Johnson's down with the flu, Smithy's wife's having a baby, Roberts has been chasing hi-jackers for the last thirty-six hours, Fennel's on a course, and that leaves you. The car'll pull up outside that sin palace of yours in approximately two minutes so get your trousers back on ready for it. They'll brief you in the car."

Quiet dignity, it's the only way. "My trousers are on, sir!"

"God, Friday night, at your age; you must be slipping!"

Friday night. Sergeant Bruton of the Birton Police Force was at home, with a prospect of a week-end off duty, his wife looking after him. Makes you laugh, doesn't it, all the nonsense they talk about loving wives and how a husband should help in the home, part of a team, giving and taking, dashing about wearing a washing-up apron? If Sergeant Bruton should ever try to get within five yards of the kitchen sink, his wife'd think him out of his senses. That's the way she wants it; that's how she sees marriage. Sergeant Bruton doesn't object. He can't change a light bulb or mend a fuse, doesn't own a Black and Decker, wouldn't know where to start with a burst pipe, or a dripping tap. Knock a nail in the wall to hang his framed commendation, and he'd bring down the plaster. She loves him for it. He was sitting by the fire, Master of the Household, Keeper of the Keys. She'd brought his slippers; by his elbow was his pipe, matches, tobacco, ashtray, the *TV Times* and the *Radio Times*. The light behind him had been switched off so's not to reflect on the screen. "Supper in ten minutes, love?" she asked, anxious to please. "You could have it sooner if you're hungry?"

"What's it to be, fish and chips?" He loved to tease her.

"The day I offer you fish and chips on your own table, you can look for a housekeeper!"

"Then, what *are* we having?"

"A nice piece of plaice, and some fried potatoes."

He grunted approval, settled back in the chair. Good to get his boots off. He could have worn shoes, of course, most of 'em did, but he'd been brought up to boots. Shoes were for the week-end, like a trilby hat, and coloured waistcoat. He heard the rustle as she unfolded the table-cloth. She touched his shoulder as she passed him, friendly, comforting. A woman's touch. He'd have a bath tonight, and when he'd done, she'd use the water. Careful like that, she was, wouldn't even draw herself a bathful of fresh water, to save him the expense. One in a million. Five minutes doze, plaice and chips, home fried the way he liked 'em, watch the television, have his bath then lie warming the bed waiting for her. Grand night, Friday, a night you were glad to be married. He yawned.

Her touch, light on his shoulder. "Go on, have five minutes," she said, "I can hold off the supper." Good lass, always cared.

The telephone rang. She put her hand on his shoulder, went to answer it. They kept it in the hall; since the police paid for it she didn't think it proper to have it in the room, to enjoy with their own possessions. "I'm not sure," he heard her say, then "I'll see if he's about." That'd be Tom from the bowls club, wanting to talk about next Tuesday's agenda. Worry guts. Jim Bruton had had the agenda typed for a week, seven copies. She came into the sitting room, closing the door carefully behind her.

"It's Inspector Aveyard," she said, "I still can't get over how young he sounds."

Friday night and the black police Humber slides inconspicuously through traffic, roof light out, travelling fast. Everybody else is going to or from pleasure, worrying about missing the best bits. Pub lights are on, waiters count their change and tuck in the cuffs of their shirts. Clean one tomorrow for Saturday, make this one do for the night. They're wringing out man-made sponges, square cut to wipe tops of plastic tables. It's a June night and clear and Aveyard's thirsty, but the pub signs don't attract him, nor does tasteless beer brewed standard so's not to offend. "Where do they all come from?" Aveyard asked the driver. He didn't answer, slipped down into third gear, touch of acceleration, and round a struggling 1100. "Snotty bugger," the driver of the 1100 mouths at them. Aveyard sits in the back, stony faced. The radio's chattering away, briefing him, covering the awkward moment between being a horny civilian with nothing but sex on his mind, and a quiet, dispassionate, disinterested officer of the law, with a job number and a possible murder on his hands.

A jaw-bone has been found; forensic has it, bridging the gap between tea and supper. The jaw-bone's human beyond a doubt, a human jaw-bone means a human corpus and the unavoidable suspicion of a crime. The Chief delegates his responsibility to Aveyard, but is never far away. "They've found the jaw-bone of a human, and the preliminaries suggest it comes from a child." The Chief's talking on the telephone from his home; they've plugged his quiet voice into an air link and Aveyard listens in his car. When they found it the bone looked fresh but that doesn't mean anything, does it? Coffins and shrouds rot faster than bones; acid and alkali leach the wood to cellulose pulp no matter how many penny a week premiums paid for it. Flesh becomes organic matter so quickly, carried by bacteria or osmosis into microscopic earth tunnels, adding vital humus to soil to fertilise the ground. But what rots wood and disseminates flesh can scour bones, preserving them clean, fresh, and anonymous throughout aeons of time.

Forensic has the bone; they'll worry it all night, that's their job. Aveyard's job is to cover the ground, to look into blank faces, and ask the right questions.

"You're Constable Verney, right?"

"Yes." Then a hasty, forgotten 'sir' stops the glare on his sergeant's face.

"And you're Sergeant Manners?"

"Yes, sir." No hesitation; that's how he got the stripes.

"And you found the bone together?"

"In a manner of speaking, sir."

"Tell me, in detail." Detail, to Aveyard, means word by

word. Joe Verney first, in the grounds of the Hall, meeting Falstaff.

"We could go there, Inspector."

"Not yet, we'll wait until I've asked a few questions."

Sergeant Bruton's out with four constables, and four powerful torches, examining every grave in the graveyard. Looking for one that's been robbed by a dog. Gruesome work.

Aveyard had a full account of the discovery of the bone from the constable and the sergeant when Bruton came into the police station. Aveyard looked up. Bruton shook his head. Aveyard introduced him all round.

"We could look at the graveyard?" Sergeant Manners said.

"We already have," Aveyard replied. Manners whistled. "Don't waste any time,do you?"

Aveyard didn't reply. The phone rang. Verney picked it up.

"It's for you, Inspector," he said.

Aveyard took it, listened. "I'll have all four," he said finally, "but not until first light."

He turned to the constable. "Dogs," he said, "with men to handle them. Can we lock Falstaff up?"

"He's my dog. I can lock him up," Brian King said.

The constable nodded.

"Do you watch Perry Mason?" Aveyard asked Brian King.

"Yes!" Mystified. Truculent.

"Then you'll remember the bit where the D.A. always says, 'we're holding you as a material witness'? Well, I'm holding Falstaff, for the same sort of reason."

It is Friday night in the village, and all are asleep. Except the constables Sergeant Bruton has placed on duty. One where West Lodge Hill meets Church Row, another on the Green, by Five Lane Ends, and the War Memorial. Another at the junction of New Farm Road and the end of Church Row, and he's the unlucky one, since he can see the police station, and knows the fire's been left on. Joe Verney's gone to bed, Lil beside him. Nooky as a consolation for the ruined holiday. Sergeant Manners has gone back to his house in Birton Sulgrave but he won't sleep. Marina, the Rector's daughter, can't get to sleep for wondering. Aveyard is asleep in bed in a cell in the Bent police station, Bruton's in the next bunk. Both fully clothed, sleep beneath blankets earning two and nine-pence for Lil who gets an allowance for washing them. Nellie Binns in the pub is dying, though Arthur Binns, her husband aged eighty, doesn't know yet. Fran's having a mild attack, but MM is coping! Mary Cevicec, who lives in a council house towards the bottom of West Lodge Road has forgotten to take the pill the Doctor gave her, since her husband, on night shift, isn't at home to remind her. She's lying there with a smile on her face, half asleep, conceiving a child, her favourite dream. Mrs Gibbins at the Hall, who's really Miss Gibbins except medically, is painting the north wall of the Butler's pantry, broad strokes of vermillion burnt sienna, scarlet lake. Plastic pails on the floor, emulsion paint she buys cheap from a stall in Birton market. This particular painting is a vision of Icarus rising out of Hell. At least, that's the way she sees it.

Oddly enough, Icarus looks like a woman, and appears to have, in the painting, the body of a dead child clutched in her hand. The child's flesh is emaciated, and the jawbone seems to protrude. While she paints, Miss Gibbins is crying, actual tears which run down her cheeks through the splashes of emulsion paint, deep rivers of an old sorrow.

CHAPTER THREE

Sergeant Bruton woke Detective Inspector Aveyard just before dawn on the Saturday morning. Aveyard awoke quickly, despite having slept for only three hours.

"The dogs are here, Inspector, and we have the first report from the lab."

A wash basin in the corner of the cell, foot operated tap, no plug or chain, and only cold water. Aveyard cupped his hands, dashed cold water over his face. Mrs Verney had put a towel out for him the previous evening. He dried his face, cleaned his teeth with the brush from his pocket, pushed back his thick hair.

There had been a crowd in the outer office Verney used, but Sergeant Bruton had sent them outside. The smell of early morning tobacco smoke lingered. "Open a window for God's sake," Aveyard said. Bruton smiled, used to his brusqueness. The report was short, a summary of immediately available information. The jaw-bone of human origin, belonged to a child aged two years at most. Sex as yet unknown, development of child 'average', "whatever that may mean?" Aveyard complained. A tap on the door. The sergeant opened it, reached into the passageway, and brought a cup of coffee, white without sugar the way Aveyard liked it. Aveyard said "thanks," then drank it slowly, thoughtfully reading the report. He looked up at the sergeant.

"What's it this time, Jim?" he asked, leaning on experience.

"That jaw-bone could be a hundred years old!"

"Or a day. Did the sergeant take that dog, what was his name, Falstaff, to the lab?"

"Yes. They'll have done a stomach analysis by now."

"Rather them than me. Can you rustle up a slice of toast?"

"Mrs Verney's offering eggs?"

"You're joking. I only want the toast to have something in my gut if and when we find the rest of it!"

Sergeant Bruton, as usual, had a plan of action. He'd traced a map of the village on a large sheet of paper. Over the village outline he'd drawn red lines, with arrow marks, rather like a television weather forecast with cold fronts and depressions. "We could work outwards from Five Lane Ends," he said. "Four teams, since we have four dogs. One south-west, through the bungalows, Binns' Farm, and the council houses. One south-east and east for Scotia's farm and part of the New Farm; one comes north-east for New Farm itself, then on to the police station here, the woods behind, and this place they call Tolly's . . ."

"While the fourth comes north-north-east and clears the grounds of the Hall, which is where Verney found the dog anyway?"

"That's right, Inspector. Four or five hours at the most."

"And the men?"

"Eight to a party, plus a dog and handler. Sergeant Manners with one, me with another, Sergeant Richards with the third. . . ."

"And me with the fourth, in the grounds of the Hall, eh?"

"I thought that's where you'd like to be."

"Thirty-two men, eh? There'll be traffic jams in Birton a mile long this morning. Where're the boffins going to be?"

"Police surgeon standing by at home."

"Dr Samson?"

"Yes, he's on duty. Then they've found a consultant pathologist from Nottingham staying with his Mum at Birton Sulgrave, and he's standing by; we'll send a car when we need him."

"And you've got the usual?"

Sergeant Bruton twitched aside a cloth covering a box standing on the floor. It was rectangular, six feet six in length, three feet wide by eighteen inches high. Air-tight, and lined, these days, with polythene. Washable!

Four hundred and fifty souls live in Bent, but where do you start? Falstaff found a jaw-bone, but that's only the part of it. The rest of the skeleton's somewhere. Four hundred and fifty souls? Or four hundred and forty-nine, and who's the other one, lying in a shallow grave? Check the electoral roll, check the houses, see for yourself. Don't take anybody's word. "Our Mabel's visiting her Aunt Polly in Darlington." The Darlington police go out with a description, and they too check for themselves. Who's had a baby? Check the electoral roll, the Registrar, the Church for chistenings, though they don't all bother with that any more. Local information. Gossip. Life is good, women are dears, but children are easy to make, and not too easy to dispose of when they arrive unwanted. This baby was two years old so somebody loved it enough to care; two years is a long time in the life of a child and a young mother. Give 'em away at birth and they go easy, put it to the breast, hold it a few times in your arms, and losing a child can be like losing a limb. It'll be hours before they know how the child died, or when, but don't take chances.

"Where's your daughter, Mr Cattell?"

"Ingeborg? Staying the night with friends in Kettering. This is a fine time to waken me to ask a question like that!"

"She ever had any children, Mr Cattell?"

No time for tact, ask the question, hope to get an answer.

Up in the wood at Tolly's Fran and MM are asleep in the double bed. Fran's snoring, of course, often does, but MM doesn't mind. You learn to accept a person's faults, don't you, even to learn to love a person more because of them. There was a knock on the door. A sudden knock. The room was totally dark. Trees all round the house kept out moonlight. MM waited. Fran's snoring continued unabated. Sleep through a thunderstorm, Fran would. The knock again. Dark night. There's a time of night when hope ebbs, when 'who am I?' replaces 'where' or 'why'. MM slipped from the bed cautious not to waken Fran. He found his dressing gown behind the door; the cool silk reassured him. He went down the stairs too quickly, his heel not firm in his slipper. Half way down, he stumbled, fell the last couple of stairs. Oh bother; that felt like a broken finger nail. The constable standing in the doorway was attractive and quite young. "Come in, come in, I'll catch my death standing on the doorstep." Then the questions. "No we do *not* have any young ladies living here." "No we do *not* have any children living here." Really, what do the police think this is, a Home for Unmarried Mothers?

Fran hadn't moved when MM got back to bed, though the snoring, thank the Lord, had stopped. "You've got *all* the blanket," MM said, petulantly. Fran didn't hear of course; dead to the world. Really!

* * *

Dawn came and went; a flock of birds, impatient for the word go, twittered in the elms at the bottom of the drive leading to Bent Hall. Aveyard was too cold for a June morn. Dawn light revealed a thick mist that burned off in minutes. Aveyard waved his men forward, wary, slow, like the start of a hunger march. Eight men in line prod each yard of the ground, a trained dog stalking the front like a sapper looking for mines. Village secrets reveal themselves. Old letters in bushes flicker white as underwear. A pair of Wellington boots and, oddly enough, one sock. At the bottom of the grounds of the Hall a small lake had been formed by stream erosion. Rhododendron and azalea all around it and a stand of willows, ducks squawk on it arrogantly safe from guns, plops of rats and fish. In a patch of rhododendron at least eight contraceptives. Aveyard felt short of sleep, his eyes already sore from looking at men looking. Mist gone, the village was clearly revealed in gaps between the trees. Pantiled roofs, and thatch still, hell to pay on bonfire night if a rocket comes down smouldering. Bent Hall on top of the crest, views of the grounds, the lake, the rhododendron walks. At one time this grass was scythed, no brambles were left to rip incautious hands. Once too here was grace and dignity, light laughing love, hands held, troth plighted, and 'Madam will you walk and talk with me?'

"Keep your eyes peeled!" Aveyard said to no-one in particular, jerking himself out of reverie.

No-one replied.

A brooch glittered half under rotted leaves; somebody'll be glad to get that back, though doubtless embarrassed if you say where it was found. Dew on the ground, boles of trees run one side. One drop held in the centre of a wild lupin, eight leaves meeting at a point and in that point, one drop of dew more clean, more crystalline than the Koh-i-Noor diamond. Burton'd buy it. Bounty for the beautiful?

When the constable on the right flank reached the water's edge, all wheeled south-west, combing the ground by the water. In the south-west corner, where the drive came in from Grove Gardens, they crossed the stream and started north-east again, staying on the east side of the drive. Nobody talked. Eight constables spread out, woken early, sweetened for duty by overtime pay, and the knowledge they wouldn't be directing the me-first horn-hooting Birton rush hour traffic. Aveyard behind the line looked nowhere in particular, everywhere in general. The dog patrolled back and forth. How many false emergencies? A bloody beef bone, half the carcase of a chicken, a hand and arm, fingernails painted bright red, but made of Hong Kong celluloid. Pheasants too young to be gunned down by the landed gentry, partridges, mallard. Rabbits that belong to poachers; a lolloping hare waits until the last minute before flashing its whitened arse. The alsatian would have bounded after it but its handler said one word, quietly, and it re-joined the police force. The constable in front of Aveyard must have weighed sixteen stones. The whole party halted at the point where the drive curves in towards the lake. The burly constable took out yesterday's handkerchief to wipe his forehead. Aveyard smiled, the constable grinned. Over on the right someone had lighted the fire in one of the thatched cottages on Bent Hill. The smoke rose straight in the wind-free morning. A fire, in June? Send a constable, verify they're not burning bones. Beyond the cottage, in line of sight, New Farm. Douglas Minsell was in the yard spannering a tractor. Mrs Minsell came out and threw handsful of maize from a yellow plastic bucket. The chickens ran from everywhere.

"Let's get on with it," Aveyard said. In line abreast, north-east. The left-hand man put in a spike, reeled out a spool of white tape as he walked. When they wheeled at the top, he'd follow that tape back down again.

They never got to the top.

The dog was standing still, his muzzle pointing down at the ground. The handler called to Aveyard. The line stopped, every man still, exactly where he was. Aveyard had been carrying a roll of polythene. He walked forward until he was about fifteen feet from the dog then placed the polythene on the ground, and rolled it slowly forward as he advanced, treading only on the fifty-inch-wide carpet.

A pile of earth had obviously been thrown backwards by a dog's paws. The hole was about twelve inches deep. Half-way out, almost buried by dirt, were the remains of a skull. All except the jaw-bone.

Each man had been carrying a stake. They formed a silent circle, dug in the stakes, and twined tape between the eyelets. Without speaking, Aveyard beckoned to three constables and sent them to inform the other search parties. The dog handler had Rip on a short lead. Aveyard went across to the dog and patted its head. The dog smirked at him.

"You have him well trained," Aveyard said. "Give your name to my sergeant." Give your name! Mentioned by name in a report, high praise indeed. Three of those and it was practically certain you'd make sergeant if you could pass the written!

"What do we do now, Inspector?" he asked.

"We wait for the pathologist," Aveyard said, "and look for its Mum."

"Where's your wife, Mr Holdeness?" Sergeant Bruton asked.

"Stopping with 'er Mum."

"Where's your daughter Christine? Is she with her Mother? Stopping with her Grandma?"

"Where else would she be?"
"How long they been gone?"
"Coupla days."
"When are they coming back?"
"I dunno. When they feel like it, I suppose."
"Go often, do they? To stay with your wife's Mum?"
"Fairly often."

Careful, Sergeant Bruton said to himself. A statement is a statement; it only becomes a fact when it has been checked. Personal feelings don't count. Keep your mind a blank if you can, a plain pad on which statements can be written ready for checking. Humphrey Holdeness, what a name, but that's got nothing to do with you, has it. Wife's name's Samantha, what a name. Daughter Christine, aged two, but keep your mind a blank. You've got Humphrey out of bed, it's obvious he sleeps in his vest and pants and you don't like people who sleep in their vest and pants, but keep your mind a blank. And you don't like people who have pretentious names to live in mean council houses called Hersanmine, do you, Sergeant Bruton, *but keep your mind a blank.* The Inspector won't want prejudice; he'll be looking for facts he can check.

"Can I just have the name and address of your mother-in-law. Just for checking, Mr Holdeness."

"I don't remember it," he said, and slammed the door in the sergeant's face. Where's the back door? Quick, remember. An alleyway comes out in Birton Road one end, Grove Gardens the other end. The sergeant beckoned to the constable, standing at the bottom of the path leading to the gate. Council houses, four in a row, space, then four more. The constable ran round the side of the four houses, stationed himself in the alleyway.

Sergeant Bruton knocked on the door again, but there was no reply.

A man's home is his castle, the moat's full, the drawbridge raised. The sergeant beckoned to another constable.

"Watch this front door. Nobody in or out."

He went and tapped on the next door, one to which he'd already been. Mr and Mrs Hector Spraggs, two teenage daughters. Mr Spraggs having breakfast, egg on his mouth. Glimpse of the teenage daughters plastered in face make-up at that time of morning. They work in a shop. Mam, cares of the world on her shoulders, fully dressed, wearing a nylon pinny, flour on her arms at this time of morning. "Excuse me, Mrs Spraggs, I wonder if by any chance you know where Mr Holdeness's mother-in-law lives?" Miraculous; she nodded: "It's Mrs Binns, they keep the pub. Not very well just now, she isn't. Not really expected to live, they say. Samantha was a late baby, Mrs Binns must have been all of forty-five when she had her. Only one, too. Remarkable, isn't it?"

She'd have gone on for ever if one of her teenage daughters hadn't come into the hall. "Can I borrow your suede jacket, Mam?" By the time she turned back to the door, the sergeant was walking briskly down the path.

He'd checked the Binns family himself. Old man, sitting in a chair, fully dressed even at that hour of morning. "I don't go up to bed, she might want something during the night." Mrs Binns herself, not sleeping, beside her two pills she's afraid to take in case she never wakes again. Once she stood behind the bar, drinking stout diluted with lemonade, dishing out crisps and sixpenny packets of salted peanuts. Now it was doubtful the Brewery would let him keep the licence. John Scotia, "he's a good lad and I can trust him, you see," kept the pub going. Arthur Binns had been a farmer in the village but you can't make a living off fifty acres with only twelve pounds an acre from barley, nine from sheep. He sold some of the land, on the left of Bent Hill where it runs into Grove Gardens, to a builder from Birton; the other farmers never forgave him. With the money he bought the pub, and now Joe Scotia used what had been the Binns Farm buildings, and grazed what was left of the land. The final blow, for which all the village blamed Binns, came when the council took the acreage to the west of the stream by West Lodge Road and built council houses on it, flooding the village with strangers.

The sergeant listened to Arthur Binns' tale of woe, looked round the small shack behind the pub, and left Nellie Binns to die as decently as she could. There had been no trace of Samantha, nor of her daughter Christine, aged two. Only Arthur Binns, sitting in the chair, fully dressed, waiting to join his wife again, in what he hoped would be some better place.

Sergeant Bruton checked his notes again; it was all in the book, reinforcing suspect memory, Arthur Binns, Nellie Binns, all rooms checked. If there'd been as much as a cat in there, Jim Bruton would have noted it; he was that kind of policeman.

Detective Inspector Aveyard was in the grounds of Bent Hall watching the consultant pathologist at work. The police surgeon, Dr Samson, had come and gone; it wasn't properly any of his affair but, though a General Practitioner, he had an interest in the more recondite pathology and had driven across to Bent before starting his rounds of summer colds and aching backs. The consultant pathologist was loading the box, removing the soil from each bone before naming it, brushing as carefully as if the remains belonged to Neanderthal Man, or an Anglo-Saxon pot. The photographer listed each bone as the pathologist named it and took a photograph, each bone was lifted, examined, wrapped in polythene, and placed in the box. Already twenty were in there, with many more to come. "Femur," the pathologist said, "leg bones." Photographed, wrapped, and packed.

The pathologist had supervised while the site was prepared. The turf had been lifted back from the edges of the hole Falstaff had scraped, then the soil was removed carefully with a large trowel. Each trowel full of soil was sifted before being stacked on a polythene sheet. Aveyard examined one of the turves. There appeared to be a flower stem stuck in it, with a withered flower head. He pulled the flower stem, and it came out of the turf, planted without roots. 'Now who the devil would want to do that,' he asked no-one in particular, "plant a flower without roots?"

Aveyard saw Bruton enter the Hall gates, walk up the drive. The sergeant came and stood beside the inspector, watching the pathologist at work. Then silently, "One child missing, aged two," he said so that only Aveyard could hear him.

The pathologist lifted one of the bones after they had taken the photograph, held it for Aveyard and the Sergeant to see.

"That'll help you!"

Aveyard looked at the bone. It didn't mean a thing. The pathologist took up another. "And so will this," he said. The gleam in his eye was that of a professional condescending to an interested amateur. "This is the ilium, what *you'd* call the pelvic bone, and this you'd call the pubic bone." Aveyard bent forward more closely to look at them, but a bone's a bone without seven years of anatomy.

"Without going into too much detail, Doctor, how will they help us?"

"They tell you the subject was a small and probably very young girl!" The sergeant looked at Aveyard.

"About two years old?" he asked.

The pathologist nodded. "You've been very lucky," he said as he bent down and went back to work with his brush, coaxing the soil granules on to his wide-bladed spatula. "Without those bones you might have had difficulty. Thank God that dog wasn't hungry!"

She waited until the police had left the grounds of the Hall, then stepped down the path from the bridge, crossed the grass to where the shrubs started. A weigelia gone mad, two enormous buddleia blooming early, long torches of purple bloom nodding like wise men asked to make a decision.

Inside the shrubberies she walked a path worn by many feet then turned, almost into the belladonna, the deadly nightshade.

"Been deadly for *me*, you devil," she said aloud.

She bent beneath the shrub and there they were, heavy navy blue cotton—passion killers they called them in school. Her name was sewn inside them on a printed tape.

"Thank God the dog didn't get this far," she thought, "he'd have gone mad!"

CHAPTER FOUR

It usually works. Loud knock. "Open up, in the name of the law." Aveyard banged on the door of Mr Holdeness's council house HERSANMINE. Knocked again. Sergeant Bruton behind him, constable at the gate. Two constables at the back guard the lane. Neighbour's curtains twitch. No sign of life from within. Aveyard knocks a third time, and this is the last! Sergeant worried; you can't break in a door without a warrant. Ought not to, anyway, though sometimes they do! Relief as he heard the shuffle of footsteps on the other side of the door. Wood's that thin, it's a wonder Aveyard's knuckles hadn't gone straight through. No knob on the outside of the door, one lock low down that twelve million keys'd fit. A letter flap of chrome, already rusted. A crack in the brickwork, and the lintel has dropped at least a quarter of an inch. There'd be a gale howling through that, come September.

The door opened. Humphrey Holdeness in grey polonecked sweater, jeans frayed at the bottoms, once brown shoes with a silver chain across the front. Thick black hair, whiskers, cigarette in his petulant mouth. Age thirty, height five eleven, weight eleven stones, distinguishing marks—a mole on his right cheek low down; Sergeant

Bruton ticked off the dossier statistics. But what about the other vital facts, the bits that go on the back of the card. Alcohol consumption brackets estimated weekly average brackets, history of violence, please specify, weapons preferred if any please specify. What is he, a knifer, a bicycle chain, knee up quick, or forehead banged forward, a mean trick. Aveyard's foot in the door, knees close together, good lad for his age and careful. "Where's your wife, Mr Holdeness?"

"We know she's not with your mother-in-law," the sergeant added. Aveyard's shoulder on the door while the sergeant's distracting Holdeness' attention, door back, Aveyard forward, inside the tiny hall-way too close for mayhem. "He's a good lad," the sergeant thought, approving the neat move.

"She's gone away for a few days," Holdeness said. Voice quiet, no trace of truculence. Know's the game's up, no point in lying. Panic before, didn't know how to react when the sergeant said, "We'll check."

"Where's she gone?" Aveyard this time. He and the sergeant, in tandem, done it before.

"Come in here," Holdeness said, and led the way into the front room. It had been used for the child. There was a cot in the corner, nappies on a brass fireguard. Three piece suite in brown uncut moquette. Piles of washing in both chairs. *Reveille*, *TV Times* and a strip cartoon book on the sofa. A matt finished table, teak veneer a millionth of an inch thick over the glued sawdust furniture-makers call wood, cockled where she'd forgotten the iron. A picture on the wall, green tinted face and shoulders of what could have been a Malayan girl. Cocktail cabinet with three bottles of stout and Sandemans Port. Football pools on the mantelpiece behind an electric clock taken from a motor car, a record player in the corner that must have cost ninety quid new and had cigarette burns on the edges of the lid.

A pile of single play forty-five records. Holdeness stood in front of the fireplace, leaning against the fireguard. Aveyard and the sergeant filled the room, all ten feet square. "Why the interest all of sudden in my wife?"

"Routine investigations, Mr Holdeness, nothing more at this stage," Bruton said.

"I see your people knocking on all the doors."

"That's right, routine investigation."

"Not just *my* wife?"

"Everybody in the village."

"Where is she?" Aveyard interrupted.

"Well, I'm afraid I've got to come out with it, straight, but you see, the fact of the matter is . . ."

"She's left you, Mr Holdeness, is that it?"

The sergeant. Mind like a computer, eyes like a microscope. Two nappies in that cot by the smell have been there a couple of days. This room may not be Mrs Bruton's idea of clean, but at least it shows some signs of housewifely pride, and no mother would leave two stinking nappies actually *in* a cot, would they?

"Wives do leave their husband sometimes, Mr Holdeness, and we can understand your pride being a bit damaged."

"Third bloody time," Holdeness said, his civility thin as the table veneer, "and this time she can come back on her bloody hands and knees and I'll not have her!"

Book out, pencil ready. Aveyard saw the pad flick. 'Lick the pencil and I'll brain you,' he thought, good humouredly.

"When did she go?" Bored voice simulated.

"Tuesday."

"Take the baby?"

"Yes."

"What time of day did she leave?"

"Musta been some time during the afternoon. She was here for my dinner, we had, like a row, and when I came back at eight o'clock she'd gone."

"Where do you work, Mr Holdeness?" Stay cool.

"Driving a tractor for Mr Minnell."

"New Farm, isn't that?"

"That's right, he has the woods on West Lodge Hill."

"Where were you working Tuesday afternoon? In the village?"

"No, up West Lodge Hill cutting timber."

"So, you couldn't have seen your wife leave?"

"No, we're right in the woods, half a mile at least."

"And you say she went twice before. Where did she go, any idea? Home to her mother?" Now you can warm him up!

Holdeness shook his head. "First time, she took a bus to London, she said, stayed overnight in a place near King's Cross, and then come home again. Second time the same thing, but this time she said she went up to Manchester."

"Did you believe her?"

"Had to, didn't I?"

"Take the baby with her?"

"No, both times was before the baby was born. She was carrying it the last time, four months."

"And you've no idea where we might start looking for her this time?" Bite in now, hard. This is what counts, isn't it?

"Not the slightest, and what's more, I don't bloody care."

"Oh, come now, Mr Holdeness," the sergeant said in his most fatherly voice, "You'd want the baby back, wouldn't you?"

"It's all the same to me."

Aveyard had been looking round the room, suddenly reached his hand across to the table. There, half hidden beneath a copy of the *News of the World*, was a purse. He picked it up, opened it. "This belong to your wife?" he asked. Holdeness nodded.

"Seems unlikely she'd leave her money, her postage

stamps, her family allowances book, doesn't it?" Got him, by the shorts!

Holdeness looked at both of them, an animal suddenly trapped, face to face. The truculent confidence ran from him like water from a sponge. His chest hollowed, his head bent forward. He turned and looked towards the mantelpiece. It was a masterly performance, Aveyard thought. Now for the Olivier bit, husky voice, tears in the eye.

There *were* tears in Holdeness's eyes, and his voice *was* husky as he said, "I think she's got herself another bloke."

'Congratulations,' Aveyard thought, 'but let's try you out with this one!' He held up the flat plastic folder. Sergeant Bruton saw it, but his face remained expressionless. "If she has gone with another bloke," Aveyard said, "she intends to behave herself!" Holdeness turned. "What do you mean?" he asked.

Aveyard drew the card from the black plastic folder. Gold one side, amber the other, with days printed on the amber side in English and French. "She can't be intending to be unfaithful to you. She's left behind the Pill."

Holdeness grabbed forward, found his forearm gripped by the sergeant. Aveyard withdrew the card fully. "And, strange though it may seem, since she left on Tuesday you say, the pill is missing for Wednesday, *and* for Thursday. Taking 'em yourself?" he asked. The sergeant let go of Holdeness's arm. He rubbed it for a moment, then suddenly he bolted. Now it was the sergeant's turn to find his arm gripped. "Learn to delegate, Jim," Aveyard said, "Let the constables do a bit of work, for a change."

They heard the door slam open, the scuffle of footsteps along the concrete path. Only when the gate had banged did Aveyard go to the front door. The two constables had converged on Holdeness; though they weren't actually holding him, he was unable to move forward without pushing them. And that, as they all knew, could constitute an assault.

"Ask him if he'd like to come up to the station with you," Aveyard suggested. Holdeness made a break for it, tried to squeeze between one of the constables and the hedge. The constable caught Holdeness's wrist as he went past, pivoted on the balls of his feet, brought Holdeness's arm smoothly up his back. There's nothing a weedy lad can do when a well-built copper has him in that grip. Aveyard signalled with his hand; the two coppers marched Holdeness up through the village to the police station.

Aveyard turned, went back inside the house. The sergeant was waiting for him in the sitting room, a smile on his face.

"That gives us a good chance to look through this place without him breathing down our necks all the time . . ."

"Without a search warrant?" Bruton said. "Whatever would the Chief say?"

CHAPTER FIVE

Saturday morning the village winds itself up for the week-end. Scotia's up early of course, but he can never sleep after five o'clock, winter or summer. Doug Minsell's been out since dawn and so has his wife Sarah; they go to bed every evening at nine, except when he's got a gleam in his eye and then its eight. Once upon a time Arthur Binns was one of the earlies with the two other farmers, but not any more. Once upon a time the Binns family farmed west of West Lodge Road, a thousand acres. When Binns' great-grandfather wanted to plough grass land he held on lease, Josiah Bent threatened to horsewhip him for his presumption and, come the next quarter day, refused to renew the lease. Binns was left with fifty acres. Josiah planted the west land with ash, elm, chestnut, poplar, and oak, but such is divine justice in the natural order of things that pheasants, grouse, partridge refused to nest there.

Doug Minsell had two lads working for him, Holdeness who married Binns' daughter, and Paul Redditch whose family had always worked at the Hall. Paul married Amy Scotia and went to live in the cottage which overlooks the green, thatched, no hot water, outside lavatory at the back. Doug Minsell could have got a grant to modernise the cottage, but Amy said she'd rather have a spare bedroom than a bathroom. 'Always wash yourself in front of the fire, can't you?" she said. Samantha Holdeness, Binns as she was, was always considered above herself; by rights she and her husband should have moved into the cottage next door to the Redditch's when they married; she had her sights on the pub and any money her father might leave, and a council house would do her to wait in. When the village saw her husband Humphrey marched to the police station between two constables, the general opinion was that Samantha had got what was coming to her.

Still, it gave a good start to the Saturday! Doug Minsell had two daughters, Cheryl and Amanda, and they had two horses, Gladys and Heidi. Heidi was Russian crossed Arab and could leap like a gazelle, Gladys was thick in the hock and in the brain, but would make a good brood mare. Cheryl and Amanda were already riding when the police brought Humphrey up New Farm Road to the police station.

"What's he done?" Cheryl called, cheeky.

Neither constable replied. Humphrey himself looked stonily forward. "What's the matter, Humphrey," Amanda called, "your television licence run out or something?" Then she wheeled Gladys away from the fence, cantered her towards a three-foot jump, three feet on a three feet spread. "Come on, old girl, up you come," she whispered. Gladys saw the jump, her ears went back, and without pause in her cantering stride, she went through the middle of the lot. Poles, wings, brush, all went flying. Amanda reined Gladys angrily to a halt, turned her round. Cheryl was sitting Heidi, neat as a pin, laughing her head off and then, when she saw Amanda had halted, she dug in her heels. Heidi leaped forward into an immediate canter, came up to the wreckage of the jump, a touch of Cheryl's whip behind the saddle, and Heidi leaped like a bird, clearing the brush, the poles, the wings, the lot. "Show off!" Amanda shouted, "bloody show off," and galloped Gladys up towards the top of the paddock.

"What's the charge?" Sergeant Manners asked, when they took Humphrey into the police station, and locked him in the cell in which Aveyard and Sergeant Bruton had slept.

"Not up to us, Sergeant, is it?" the constable said, "we weren't there at the time. All we know is the inspector and the sergeant went into this house, and after a few minutes this fellow came dashing out. We grabbed him, and brought him here."

"Section 51?"

"Could be, obstructing a police officer in the execution of his duty; but then again, it could be an assault, if the sergeant gets here with a black eye, couldn't it?"

"I never hit nobody," Holdeness protested, through the barred door.

"You don't have to hit anybody," the sergeant said, "it's enough just to touch 'em. Now, how would you like to stay quiet there, drink a cup of tea and wait until we hear what the inspector has to say."

House to house search again, but this time, go round quickly before they leave for work. "Have you seen Samantha or Christine Holdeness? If so, when and where? When was the last time you saw her, when and where?" Write it all down. Sergeant Bruton was good at that sort of thing, a neat orderly almost computerised search. Every statement checked, and cross checked. "You saw her going into the shop on Tuesday evening?" Make a note to check the shop.

"Oh, you misbegotten son of a papist whore-monger,"

Sam Gainer said, as Aveyard walked into his shop shortly after ten o'clock on Saturday morning. "What the hell brings you to Bent?" Then, "Cluney," he called. "Guess who's come!" 'Cluney', Miss Clunes as was before Sam married her, waddled into the shop from the back quarters. "Bill," she exclaimed, her pleasure obvious, "what are *you* doing here?"

"Working, I'm sorry to say!"

They were all silent. Bill Aveyard had met Sam Gainer and Miss Clunes when he went to investigate a murder in the village in which Sam kept the post-office. It was an unhappy memory. Since then they had met several times, and Aveyard had attended the wedding as a witness. "You only do murders," Sam said, "don't tell me there's been one in Bent?" He grasped Cluney's hand. "Anyway," he added, "first things first. Have you had any breakfast, have you time to stop and have a cup of coffee, and come inside, for God's sake." He lifted the counter flap and Aveyard went through into the back room. He sat down in an easy chair by the window, overlooking the garden and Scotia's farm. "I haven't a lot of time, and I do have a couple of official questions to ask you." Sam Gainer slapped Cluney's rump. "You heard him," he said, "get him a cup of coffee while he asks his questions." Cluney left the door into the kitchen open so she could hear.

"It's an odd case," Aveyard said, "so far in two parts which may or may not be connected. Firstly, we've found some bones we believe to be human, and secondly, we suspect a woman and her child are missing."

"And you don't want me to jump to conclusions?"

"No, I don't. The woman and her child are Samantha Holdeness and her daughter Christine."

"Good Lord," Cluney said from the kitchen door.

"Coffee!" Sam said, firmly.

"It's on the stove."

"Then get it off the stove and into the cups!"

"All our reports so far show Mrs Holdeness as having been in here late on Tuesday. Can you give me any details?"

"Hang on a minute," Sam said. From the shelf above the fireplace he produced a ledger, bound in red cloth. He opened it. "Tuesday?"

"Late."

"That's right," Sam said, "Forty cigarettes. She was the last in, or anyway, she was the last to get credit. She must have been in about half past seven. Fran before her." He held the book open for Bill Aveyard to see. Each person obtaining credit had his name and the purchase entered in the book, in sequence. Aveyard flipped the pages. Three leaves back he found the heading in Sam's neat writing, Tuesday, 8th June. First entry D. Minsell, one ounce of Cut Golden Bar. A roster of the village names, then Fran, last entry Mrs Holdeness, forty Woodbine tipped. A neat line ruled across the page, and the entry on the next leaf, Wednesday 9th June. First entry, Scotia, quarter pound of mintoes and a pair of leather boot laces. Aveyard ran his eye down the pages for Wednesday, Thursday, Friday, Saturday. D. Minsell had been in this very morning for Cut Golden Bar, and Scotia had been in for mintoes. "Twice a week, regular as clockwork, Scotia has his mintoes," Sam Gainer said.

"Did Mrs Holdeness buy her cigarettes always in forties?" Sam riffled through the pages, then "hang on a minute, I'll get her own book." Mrs Holdeness's book was bright red, six by four. "Your Sergeant Bruton'd be proud of me," he said, with a restrained chuckle, "he on this with you?"

"Flanagan and Allen."

Sam Gainer's finger ran down each of the last three completed pages in the book. "Interesting," he said, and handed the book to Bill Aveyard. Aveyard examined it; "Comes in more or less every day, doesn't she?"

"Yes, and gets cigarettes."

"But only ten, ten at a time, every day."

"Yet on Tuesday evening, she comes in for forty."

Cluney came in from the kitchen, three coffee cups on a tray. "You take milk but no sugar if I remember," she said smiling, proud of her memory. He nodded, thinking about cigarettes. Sam Gainer was watching him. "The temptation must be great in police work to jump to conclusions," he said.

"Ten cigarettes a day, a habit, then, forty cigarettes and hasn't been in since. You could say she was laying in a small stock; but then, equally well, you could say she was having a party, or that her husband, who smokes, had asked her to bring a packet for him. Does he buy cigarettes here?"

Sam shook his head. "In the pub, I imagine. Comes in early sometimes for eggs and bacon, when she's forgotten, a quarter of lard, butter, things like that, but never cigarettes."

Cluney was sipping her coffee, put down the cup. "Do you want gossip, Bill, or would you rather not?"

"Anything is useful, at this stage."

"She's left him before, they say. They also say he was having a fling with Mrs Cevicec, though what he could see in her. . . ."

"*Miaoaw!*" Sam said, not unkindly.

"No, not that, but she's had four children . . ."Suddenly she realised her own present condition. "They say you lose your looks when you've had a family . . .", she said, looking at Sam.

Sam's eyes shone at her. New love, old love. He'd been married before, but his first wife died. Cluney and he had lived together for years. In a sense Bill Aveyard exposed that relationship when Miss Clunes, as she then was, had given Sam Gainer an all-night alibi in a murder case Aveyard was investigating.

"That's your cue to say something nice . . ." Aveyard said.

"What, and give the lady ideas above her station . . ." Cluney aimed a gentle blow at him but he ducked. Love play doesn't change whatever the age of the players.

"Samantha Holdeness," Aveyard asked, "what was *she* like. Attractive?"

"Humphrey must have thought so," Cluney said.

"Unless he was marrying into a pub." Sam was always a cynic of sorts, or liked to pretend he was. "I would say she was attractive enough, if you like 'em a bit heavy, coarse, sensual, you know what I mean. Some men go for that type. She'd a hard edge to her tongue, I can tell you that. I'll bet she was a shrew to live with!"

"You're using the past tense, Sam," Cluney said, "jumping to conclusions."

"Mrs Cevicec, what's she like?"

"Oddly enough, now you come to ask, very much the same sort of woman, a bit heavy, definitely coarse, sensual."

"And the baby, anything special about Christine?"

Both looked at him, in consternation. "Haven't they told you?" Cluney asked, amazed.

"Told me what?"

Cluney grasped Sam's hand, gripping tight. Sam held her reassuringly.

Sam looked at Cluney, moved his coffee forward on the tray, fiddling with the spoon. "Cluney's been a bit worried since we're having a baby late in life, but Dr Samson keeps telling her there's no need to worry. You know how women are! We should have had the baby sooner, I suppose, or we shouldn't have one at all, but we both want it and Dr

Samson's keeping a very careful watch on Cluney, all the time."

"It isn't easy, Bill, when you hear about some babies born of older parents! I'm over forty, you know, and well, with that terrible thing happening even to such a young healthy pair as the Holdenesses. . . ."

"What was wrong with their baby?" he asked, gentle as he could be. "She was born without legs," Sam said.

CHAPTER SIX

On the corner, where New Farm Road joins Church Row, and almost opposite the police station, Horst Cattell had his wood-yard. His grandfather came over from Denmark on one of the first butter boats, walked inland from Lowestoft, liked the trees of Bent and stayed. For a while he worked for Minsell, then applied for a contract to cut chestnut stakes in the woods on West Lodge Hill. As soon as he had a good business in chestnut fencing, he learned enough English to ask one of the Minsell girls (there were seven in those days) to marry him, and settled down in a cottage on the corner. Trees had always been his passion and he'd spent many years of his youth in the forests of Norway, above Bergen. Josiah Bent's son and heir, Albert George Henry, recognised his abilities, and gave him responsibility for maintaining all the woods around Bent. He rented six acres of land on the corner, bought a steam engine and saws, and set up as a timber merchant. By the time Horst Cattell inherited the business in 1935, the steam engine had been replaced by diesel, the whole of that corner was covered in well-matured trunks, and the Cattell business had acquired a reputation for best English Oak. They deserved it; some of their trunks had matured for upwards of a hundred years. Horst, when he came into the business, married Rowena Densford whose father was a self-employed carpenter in a small way in Birton. They had two children and Horst maintained the Scandinavian tradition of his family by calling them Ingeborg and Flemming. Both worked in the timber yard with their father, and he would have no other employees.

A saw yard is a dangerous place, and Horst's safety precautions, to say the least, were primitive. "It'd take a year to teach anybody new," he once said, "and by that time they've lost a finger, a hand, or an arm." Working in the wood-yard Ingeborg had lost nothing. Out of doors in all weathers, or under the corrugated iron roof of the saw shed, she was deft and nimble as Horst himself, making up in skill what she lacked in sheer brute strength, though she was no weakling. To see her handle a bar and move a twelve-foot by twenty-four-inch diameter tree trunk on the bed of the three-foot circular saw was a study in movement; she used infinitely less energy than her brother Flemming, achieved twice the amount of work. Rubber boots, jeans, a polo-necked jumper, winter or summer, she never missed a day. The saw yard had five saws, one six feet circular for cutting trunks down their lengths, one a band saw nine feet high for slicing tree thrunks along the length into planks, a third for chopping cord wood and bark into logs for firewood, and a fourth pre-set to cut pit-props and billets from which Cattell made his bread and butter income. The fifth was petrol driven, a small chain saw used mainly for lopping branch stubs from tree trunks. The large corrugated iron-roofed shed also contained winches for hoisting tree trunks, and gantries for bringing the trunks in from the weathering 'yard' outside. Each of these saws, and winches, Ingeborg could handle with equal facility. She weighed eight stones only, was twenty-five, had brown hair, and four steady boy-friends. Her father paid her six pounds a week and she had over a thousand pounds in the Savings Bank, all her own, all earned.

Aveyard had walked up New Farm Road; it was half past ten on Saturday morning, and already he felt he'd done a day's work. Ingeborg Cattell was working in the wood-yard, handling the tongs which dangled from the end of the mobile hoist. Her brother Flemming was in the cab. Ingeborg took the tongs on the end of the wire rope—they alone must have weighed a couple of hundred weight—and dropped them like hairclips around the two-foot trunk of an old oak. She beckoned to her brother, who let in the hoist clutch, lifted the trunk slowly into the air. The thicker end dangled on top of the pile of logs, swinging dangerously. Ingeborg nipped out of the way, pushed the trunk with a billet, swung it back in line. Flemming drove forward, dropped the trunk in the path of the gantry. By this time, Ingeborg had sped along the trunks, grabbed the tongs from the gantry, and as the trunk settled on the ground she dropped one pair on, lifted the other pair off. Then she went to the side of the corrugated-iron shed, worked the lever of the diesel machine. The belting snapped and whirled, and the trunk was slowly lifted. Then the gantry carried the trunk along, dropped it neatly on the travelling saw bed of the six feet circular. She dropped small wedges of wood on each side of the trunk to prevent it rolling, avoiding the groove where the saw cut would come, then switched off the gantry and started the circular. When the blade had reached speed, she worked the lever that started the saw table forward. It travelled slowly, a bad bearing clanking under the immense weight of the trunk. When the saw bit into the end of the trunk, the thin whine changed to a snarl as the teeth ate forward. The trunk travelled the length of the saw table to where Ingeborg and her father, Horst, were waiting with crowbars. They flipped the thinner cut piece away from the rest of the log—that'd be used for firewood—and sent the saw table back to where it had started. Crowbars again, and now the trunk flipped over, lying flat on its cut edge. No need for wedges, the trunk slid backwards and forwards being sliced into four-inch-thick sections, each about two feet wide and twenty feet long.

So interested had Aveyard been watching Ingeborg, so attracted by the sight of her manhandling the tree trunk, that he had walked into the wood-yard from New Farm Road.

Down with the hoist again, this time to move the slabs from the circular saw to the band saw, for slicing into four by fours. The girl saw him for the first time as the hoist lifted. She came across, could hardly make herself heard for the noise of the diesel engine. She smelled strongly of pine wood and shavings, the fresh odour after-shave lotion manufacturers imitate but can't copy.

"All right to use the cross cut?" she asked.

Aveyard was mystified. She saw the look on his face.

"Police, aren't you?" Pride injured. "How'd you know?"

"Your sergeant's been in. You must be this Inspector Graveyard he was talking about."

"Aveyard!" More injuries to his pride.

She turned round, saw Flemming crossing the wood-yard, drew her hand across her throat. Flemming understood, went into the diesel shed, and switched off, or lifted the valve, or did whatever you do to stop a diesel. The silence was awe-inspiring. In it, Aveyard heard Bruton's well-recognised cough behind him.

"How did you know to come in here, Inspector? Seen Henry?"

"No, I was just admiring the way this young lady was throwing this tree trunk about."

She smiled at him, feminine, dimpled.

"I was just looking for you, missed you in Gainer's shop. You must have come up New Farm Road. I went down Bent Hill."

"What's this young lady on about, can they use the cross cut?" The sergeant said nothing, led him across the saw yard, over a pile of cut four by fours, past a stack of four by twelves by an inch—'coffee table tops', the girl explained—to the back doors. They were at least twenty feet high and hanging, made of pieces of rejected timber and corrugated iron. Horst, it seemed, didn't approve of capital expenditure. By the door, and at right angles to it, was a twenty-inch circular saw. The flat table was mounted on a swivel so that a log could be held on the bench and a foot movement would bring it up and over. To the left of the saw table was a pile of timber, each piece four feet long, obviously the outsides of the trees, still carrying the bark. Without apparent effort, Ingeborg pulled open the twenty-foot door. Beyond it was a pile of firewood. "Useful sideline," she said.

A constable was standing guard, behind the saw bench, hidden from Aveyard's view by the timber. He touched his flat cap. "Wilkinson, Inspector," he said, "B Division, traffic."

"Where's your bicycle?" the inspector asked. It was a Birton joke, a greeting, no more.

"One of the dog handlers, before he went off duty, thought he'd take the opportunity to come in here and price a bit of timber for a shed he's building," the sergeant said. "He lives in Burton Latimer. Brought his dog with him, let it off the lead. The dog came over here while the handler was talking to Miss Cattell."—"Howdydo, pleased to meet you"—and went mad in the sawdust. Smart lad, the handler, came belting back, leaving the dog with a 'stay', and fetched the forensic boys, who'd just finished with the pathologist. They stopped the pathologist, he came here, and he's taken a bag of sawdust back with him. They sifted the whole lot, but couldn't find anything. I came looking for you, but thought they'd better get on with this quickly, put Wilkinson here to keep his eye on it, and let the forensic boys get back to Birton with the pathologist."

Aveyard bent down, picked up a handful of the sawdust. He sniffed it, nothing unusual. He threw it back on the floor, wiped his hands against his trousers leg. "They didn't find anything?"

"Nothing."

"They sent the dog all round, of course, and he found nothing?"

"Nothing, except Miss Cattell's sandwiches!"

"You owe me dinner, Inspector."

"I'll be pleased to see you get the same as I get, if I have any dinner!" She smiled at him. Dammit, he'd got a date. "You can't see anything out of the ordinary?" he asked her.

"Nothing at all."

"And from your experience, do dogs eat sawdust?"

"I've never seen one. We have a lot of trouble with cats . . ."

"Do they eat it?"

She laughed. "No, they mess in it, cover it up. You don't find it until you grab a handful, like you just did!"

Instinctively, he looked at his hands, wiped them again down his trousers. She laughed again. Really, that was a lovely laugh she had! Dinner would be a pleasure.

"Is it all right to use the cross saw?"

Aveyard looked at the sergeant, then shook his head. "Do you mind waiting," he said, "until I've had a word with our people?"

She beckoned to Flemming, who went into the shed. The diesel engine laboriously started again, clump clump clump.

"See you at half past twelve," she said.
"I don't suppose I'll have heard by then . . ."
"But I'll be hungry . . ." she said, laughing again.

CHAPTER SEVEN

Detective Inspector Aveyard, and Detective Sergeant Bruton walked slowly out of the wood-yard, up New Farm Road, round the corner into Church Row, into the police station. Neither spoke. Constable Verney was in the police office, standing up at the counter, the daily ledger open in front of him. When he saw them come in, he straightened up. "Sergeant Manners says I'm to stay on duty as long as required!"

"Yes, I suppose you'd better. Sorry about your holiday; can you make arrangements a bit later?"

"Have to, won't we, Inspector?"

Watch it, Bill said to himself. Detectives are used to work taking precedence; after a year or two a village copper gets into a time-on time-off routine he hates to break.

"You got a round, lad?" Sergeant Bruton asked, sensing Aveyard's restraint.

Verney glanced up at the clock. "Starts in three minutes, Sergeant."

"Then you've got three minutes to pump up your tyres, haven't you?"

Verney got the message, glanced at Aveyard, took up his

helmet, saluted, and left. Aveyard went behind the counter, glanced at the neat handwriting on the daily log. The page was almost filled. He flipped back. Yesterday only had seven lines all day. He sat in the armchair, looking at nothing but the wall. The sergeant walked across the tiny office, sat on the hard chair by the table, looked at the clutter of papers, official instructions in bound books, pamphlets, note books, statement books. He lifted the suitcase he always brought with him on these jobs, opened it, took out the map with which he'd searched the village, spread it out.

"Did the pathologist give you a time?" Aveyard asked.

"No, Inspector." A brief answer, but Aveyard didn't want a lot of chatter. He'd talk when he had a mind to, not before.

The phone rang. The sergeant picked it up, listened, put it down. Picked it up again then, "Sergeant Bruton," he said. He listened for about ten seconds, said "thank you," and put the instrument back on its cradle.

"That was Constable Verney," he said, "ringing from the Green, his first point. He said to remind you there's a man in the cells, and he hasn't yet been charged!"

"Oh damn," Aveyard said, "so there is. I'd forgotten all about him!" The sergeant opened the wooden door; behind it was the grilled door of the cell. Holdeness was asleep. The sergeant sprang the lock, turned the key, removed the bar, and the door swung open. It took him some time to waken Holdeness, who was mumbling in his sleep. When he came awake, he blinked at the sergeant.

"She come back then?" were his first words.

"Up lad," the sergeant said, "and out here."

"Is there a . . .?"

"Use the bucket. And don't forget to put the lid back on!" When Holdeness came through to the office, he'd not only used the bucket, but the wash basin too. And he'd combed his hair with his fingers.

"Where is she," he asked, "waiting at home?"

Aveyard bounced from his chair, snarling. "No, she's not!" he said, grasping the front of Holdeness's polo-necked sweater. "What did you say down there, 'it's all the same to me', and you with a daughter with no legs! What kind of a sod are you, anyway."

He let go of the polo sweater. He'd felt Jim Bruton's hand in the small of his back, warning him, restraining him, advising him. Aveyard went back, sat down in the arm chair. "Get him out of my sight, Sergeant Bruton, as fast as you can. And get the NSPCC on to it; file a *Missing Persons*. Yes, and inform the Salvation Army because it's a certain fact that bugger won't!" Sergeant Bruton bustled Holdeness out of the office into the yard outside the police station, shut the door behind him. Aveyard slumped there, still fuming. That baby and its mother needed all the help and human sympathy they could get; they were tied to a lout, rumoured to be having it off with another woman, mother of four!

When Bruton came back into the office he too looked angry. "I got the story from Holdeness," he said. "It makes you sick, doesn't it?" Aveyard had seen his car outside, radio and driver. Holdeness would be sitting in the back and the driver passing the details to Birton. Within hours they'd have NSPCC and Salvation Army looking for her, and every constable on a beat anywhere in England would have a description. The police don't look for missing persons unless a felony is suspected, but somewhere, sometime, they'd see her and report it. Aveyard couldn't blame her running away from a husband like that.

"We're wasting our time it seems to me," he said. "What have we got? A box of old bones, and from the look of them I'd guess they've been in the ground hundreds of years, a lout whose wife has run away and left him, two missing contraceptive pills, and a dog that eats sawdust."

"You've got that look on your face," the sergeant said, smiling.

"What look?"

"Remember that cock-pit of roses, and the girl who wasn't raped? You had it on your face that time. No case to answer, but something that doesn't smell right."

"It's that bucket Holdeness has been using!"

"Thirty, forty, fifty years ago, they'd have dug up the bones, buried 'em again in the Churchyard, and nobody would have been any wiser. Now we mount a full-scale investigation before we get the pathologist's report . . ."

"What would we think if we'd done nothing for six, ten hours, and the pathologist reported the bones had only been in the ground for a couple of days. Whoever'd put them there could be in Australia on ten quid!"

"You said yourself they looked as if they'd been in the ground hundreds of years. That's what I thought!"

"But we could be mistaken. Depends on the ground, doesn't it. In some ground a corpse can stay more or less as it is, preserved, for years. Other ground, it rots within weeks. What's the matter, you're looking a bit green!"

"It's all right for you young lads with strong stomachs," Bruton complained. "And talking about stomachs, what about your dinner date?"

"You hold the fort?"

"I'll have that egg I didn't fancy for breakfast. You'll be at The Green Man, I suppose?"

"Not on your nellie. A girl like that deserves steak and chips!"

"The Trumpet? Spreading it, aren't we? And I guess her old man doesn't give her luncheon vouchers, neither!"

There weren't many people in The Trumpet on Saturday for lunch. Outside Birton, near the shoe manufacturers and leather tanners, The Trumpet did a strong week-day trade, clerks from the offices fed up with sandwiches came there for steak pie chips and a pint of beer for four and sixpence. Makes a change, when you've got the money. Aveyard could claim ten bob a day subsistence allowance on a job, and ordered steak and chips, cheese and coffee. Ingeborg, after some persuasion, ordered the same, with a gin and tonic. She'd wanted a half pint of bitter, but Aveyard wasn't in that mood. There was chicken on the menu, and veal cutlets, both at six and six pence. He'd ordered the veal, was surprised when she looked disgusted. "I'll never eat veal," she said, "and neither would you if you thought about the way they get it!"

"Chicken?"

"Broiler birds, locked up all their lives, light switched on in the middle of the night to make them lay another egg!"

"You've no objection to steak, I hope?"

"I wish I was strong enough," she said, "to be a complete vegetarian and not eat meat of any kind . . ."

"We could always sit in the back of the car, share a bag of peanuts and drink a glass of milk. No, come to think of it, you'd draw the line at milk, too; fruit juice, I suppose?"

"I'm not cranky, you know, it's just that some things seem so cruel to me. Anyway, let's forget it, and tell me some more about being a detective inspector. You look so young for a job with so much responsibility. I mean, I always thought of them as . . ."

". . . having one foot in the grave?" She laughed again, honest, open, sincere. Wholly delightful, Aveyard thought, and such a refreshing change. Obviously intelligent, but not 'academic', she'd thought about things, formed her own opinions. In a wood-yard you'd either turn into a zombie, as her brother probably had, or you'd think independently, nothing second hand.

"Being younger than most of 'em does give me awful

problems. Nobody ever takes me seriously."

"That could be an advantage. I imagine you're the sort could sneak up on a person; I'd hate to be questioned by you. I wouldn't know what I was saying until I'd said it, and then it'd be too late."

"It does have its advantages, I must admit."

The waiter, who knew him, came across without the coffees. "You're wanted on the telephone," he said, tactfully not using the title of Inspector.

"The path. report's in," Bruton said on the telephone, "shall I read it out to you? It's not long."

"Not unless it's urgent. I'll come back." The important thing about the path. report was not the actual words used, but a feeling you get when you read between the lines. Pathologists are careful people by nature.

"Feels very grand," Ingeborg said, as she settled back in the seat of the Humber, behind the police driver. "I hope nobody thinks you're arresting me?" "If I were to lock you up," Aveyard said, smiling, "it wouldn't be in a police cell!" Language of flirtation, overtones, undertones. Why could two people never say, as soon as they felt the mutual attraction, "Look here, I like you, I think you might like me, what about getting to know each other?"

"I'd be safer in a police cell!" she said.

"But it'd be less interesting . . .?"

"Now who's boasting!" Pheasants do it, a dance of love, bright plumage and chest ruffles. Trees need wind to cross-pollinate them. Humans use sight and sound and fail to achieve the simple success of pheasants or trees.

"We'll have to try it some time," he said.

"Chance would be a fine thing!" Even a female pheasant jibs sometimes, trees band against the wind. The wise cock waits, the tree stands stately. The cock crows, however, sometimes!

"You'd better stand by when we get to Bent," Aveyard

said to the drvier, "I may need you again, I just don't know until I've seen the pathologist's report."

"Very good, sir," the driver said. Ingeborg was suitably impressed.

Aveyard was silent until they came in sight of Bent, to the right off the Birton Road. "I imagine you're busy tonight?" he asked.

"If you call reading a book busy? I imagine *you'll* be busy," she said, smiling.

"I haven't had time to get to the library, so I haven't a book to read. Maybe I could read yours with you?" he asked. In the mirror, he saw the driver smile, smiled himself, so completely had she dissipated his earlier bad humour. "I've got a copy of Moriarty's Police Law I could lend you, sir," the driver said, catching his smile.

"I don't think he'll need it," Ingeborg said, as she climbed out of the car by the wood-yard.

The first pathology report was tentative, each phrase so wrapped in 'could be' and 'appears' as to be practically meaningless. It takes a sharp eye to prune the verbiage.

"That's it, then," Aveyard said, "we were wasting our time. That skeleton's been in the ground about twenty-five to thirty years. That'd make it war-time, wouldn't it? A lot of funny things happened in war-time, and I don't imagine we'd have a hope in hell of tracing it, what with the floating population. A WAAF, or an ATS girl, most likely, got herself into trouble, and dumped it."

"But why this," the sergeant said, stabbing the report with his fiinger, "why keep the baby alive for two years. Hundreds of babies are dumped every year at birth, or were during the war, on steps of hospitals, in telephone booths, but why bring up the poor little bastard for two years?"

"Simple. Look, ATS girl has an affair on camp, gets

pregnant. Has the baby, probably even in Birton hospital, with a curtain ring on her finger. Discharged from the Army of course, comes out here to live, possibly not even in this village. Father goes to the Far East, or is killed in action, mother grieves, the baby dies, mother dumps it."

"But why not in a proper cemetery?"

"I don't know why 'here'. Maybe she wanted to avoid a scandal. Maybe she did it on impulse, maybe she killed the child herself, maybe the mother was killed in action and the father dumped it!"

"Maybe the child was with foster parents, drawing a couple of pounds a week. Maybe the payments stopped, so they dumped it."

"Maybe, maybe, maybe, Jim, that's all we've got. I'll have a word with the Chief, and we'll close the case. They can give it to one of the new boys, spare time enquiry, something to do and a feeling of Pinkerton."

The sergeant put his map back into the suitcase, clipped his pen and pencil into his inside pocket. "And Mrs Holdeness," he asked, "and that poor baby?"

"Look, I feel as badly as you do about that, Jim, but we're not 'Missing Persons'. We have no reason to suspect a felony. I can understand perfectly well that she couldn't stand the sight of him, and left. I'd have done the same myself in the circumstances. She went to the shop, drew forty fags to keep her going, walked to the bus-stop, and just disappeared."

"There was no pram in that house . . ."

"You noticed that, too, did you? They'll find the pram, or she's taken it with her."

"It'd be a pram, not a push chair?"

"A pram I reckon."

"What about the pills?"

"Well, she wouldn't take 'em with her, would she. She'd be disgusted with men. The last thing she'd be thinking of would be nooky."

"Where could the two missing pills be?"

"Inside Mrs Cevicec. That bugger Holdeness is probably so stupid he thinks the Pill works like cocoa butter, fizzy foam. Makes you sick, doesn't it. He might be the one with a genetic fault, causing the kid to be born without legs. Mrs Cevicec could be in the same boat at this very moment."

"Taking a lot for granted, aren't we?"

"Why not, it's not our case. It's good to be able to speculate once in a while, knowing we don't have to bring it into court."

The phone rang. The sergeant picked it up. "Sergeant Bruton. Yes, sir," he said and handed the instrument to Aveyard. "The Chief," he hissed. Aveyard grimaced, grabbed the instrument. "Yes, Chief, Aveyard here."

"Tell your sergeant not to hiss. If he wants to disclose my identity to you, tell him to do so in a loud clear voice!"

"Yes, Chief."

"What's all this rubbish about sawdust?"

"I'm waiting for the pathologist's report, Chief. I was going to call you, later."

"Well, you won't need to, now. They called me, just when I was cutting the grass. Why is it, Detective Inspector Aveyard, that every time I set foot in my garden on a Saturday afternoon, I get a blasted telephone call that has something to do with you!"

The Chief was a fanatical two-days-a-week gardener, hated being disturbed during those days. Aveyard, a bachelor, didn't object to week-end duty, often took it to let his married colleagues spend a week-end with families, but try explaining that to the Chief! Without waiting for an answer to his purely rhetorical question, the Chief had gone on talking. "I've had a run-down on the skeleton report; no point in keeping you on a thirty-year-old skeleton case. John Freeman can start Monday, run it in with the lead stealing job he's been on for the last six months. Now, about that sawdust! No wonder the dog was eating it. It's impregnated with bone dust and blood! What do they do in that saw yard?"

Oh, Ingeborg, who won't eat veal or chicken, dour Horst Cattell, Flemming with his round smiling face.

"Human blood, Chief?"

"Too early for that. This much however they can say, it's not more than four days old, and there's a lot of it. That saw's been used recently to chop somebody or something into little pieces."

Whatever Horst Cattell lacked, it wasn't courage.

"Nobody uses our saws, Inspector, I'll swear to that. Our livelihood depends on the saws; we wouldn't let nobody touch them. One nail, that's all it takes, one nail in the trunk of a tree, and it can stop work for a day. Oh, they came here, sassy enough for anything. We've bought these railway sleepers cheap, and wonder if you could cut 'em lengthways into fencing posts, or two by twos to make greenhouse bars. And railway sleepers is the worst, nails in 'em, and stones."

"When you're not working, the saws are switched off?"

"Ask Flemming, that's his job, the diesel engine."

Aveyard *would* ask Flemming, you could rely on that. And he'd ask Ingeborg, so prim and proper she wouldn't eat veal. He glanced at Jim Bruton. What did he make of it.

"Is there any possibility those saws could be left running while you went out to bring in a tree trunk?" the sergeant asked. "Think carefully about it. We know what the saws have been used for; if you now tell us no-one else could have had access to them, we shall be forced to conclude the saw was used either by you, or a member of your family."

Horst thought about that one. Ingeborg was standing immediately behind him, Flemming to one side. Horst turned, and looked from one to the other. Aveyard looked, too. It was inconceivable that either one could have done it, could have held a body on that saw bench, worked the foot lever, and . . . it was inconceivable. Ingeborg shook her head, Flemming shook his head. "Wood," he said, "timber, that's all as has been through that saw, to my certain knowledge."

"The saws couldn't have been used while you were all away from the yard?" Aveyard asked.

Flemming reached inside the torn pocket of his jacket. A key ring was on the end of a piece of string pinned to the lining. "I kept losing it," he said, "until Ingeborg sewed it in for me. Without that, you couldn't start that engine."

Aveyard examined it. It was unlike any other he'd ever seen, an octagonal shank with flanges protruding. It'd take an engineer to copy a key like that, and he'd need plenty of time. "It fits the fuel injector," Flemming explained. "Without that in and turned, you couldn't get any fuel. Not many about now. Mostly it's bits o' pressed tin that fit into the starter box, just like a car key, a million made, all the same." Aveyard let go of it; it dangled on its length of string until Flemming tucked it back into his pocket. It was his talisman, his pride, his one bit of responsibility.

"We can prove bones have been chopped on this saw; you deny using the saw for that purpose, and you also say categorically that no-one else could have access to it, is that right?"

Horst looked at his two children for hasty and final confirmation then, "that's absolutely right," he said.

"And that," Ingeborg added, "is what I suppose you'd call an impasse."

* * *

Birton was a progressive police department, with an attentive Watch Committee prepared to appropriate adequate public funds from the rates, when necessary. In consequence, the County Chief Constable, Major Sir Roger Cockburn, had all the staff and equipment he could use. Aveyard walked up the stairs to the first floor of the Northants Mutual Society Building, just off Marefair in Birton. Not many people knew the top three floors of the building were occupied, not by Northants Mutual but by the back-room boys of the police force. A lift went from the first to the fourth; gave access to laboratories often used by the public analyst and the larger forensic department of Nottingham. Ernest Bradbury in charge had the equivalent rank of Chief Superintendent but never took off his white coat; a pink-faced pleasant man, his hobby was sailing on the gravel pits at Thrapston, or the Pitsford reservoir. His age? Impossible to say. Somewhere in the hinterland of thirty-five to forty-five. His qualifications, however, would have got him the Professorship of the Science Faculty of any of the redbrick universities. He was bending over a Zeiss multi-optic microscope when Aveyard walked across the laboratory. He straightened, rubbed his eyes, put his glasses back on. "Look at that," he invited Aveyard. Aveyard bent over the microscope, adjusted the eye-piece to his own focal length. The objective sprang into sharp focus. Low magnification, but sufficient to separate the purple strands of fibrous matter from the white jagged bone fragments. "We dyed the wood," Bradbury explained, "to make it more visible. Bone doesn't take the dye." He led Aveyard across to the polished wooden bench. There was a double rack at the back of the bench containing stoppered bottles of hydrochloric, sulphuric, nitric acid, and various alkalies. On the bench was a double gas outlet, each with a bunsen burner at the end of a short length of rubber gas-pipe. There were two tripods. Each had a gauze on it, and on the gauze were two beakers. One appeared to contain water, the other a thin milky substance. In each beaker was a stirring rod. Bradbury stirred each in turn. "This is a pilot we always run parallel with the subject we're testing. You'll see it's quite clear, no sign of precipitation. This other one, however . . ." He took the rod and stirred that one. "Calcium," he said gravely. "From bone matter."

"Human or animal?"

"We can't tell. The bone matter of animals is indistinguishable from that of humans by chemical means. If we can see the bones, often we can identify them. Each animal has bones of a specific shape, but even then we have difficulties. The bones of a monkey are very similar to human bones, though the humerus, the radius and the ulna, which make up the bones of the upper and lower arm, are usually longer in proportion to the rest of the body than human ones would be. But, *in proportion*, Inspector. And that means we have to have an almost complete skeleton for comparison!"

"So there's no help you can give me?" It was five o'clock in the afternoon. Aveyard had been on the go since dawn and felt it. He passed a hand wearily across his face. Bradbury eyed him sympathetically. These young 'uns didn't have the stamina of the older ones, but they put more of themselves into police work, burned themselves out faster. "Speaking of bones, we can tell you very little, as yet. We can get a weighed sample of the bone dust from wood matter, and subject that sample to exhaustive analysis. As a result, we shall know exactly what percentage of what elements we can find. Now, we know that the nutrition of animals and humans varies considerably, and thus we should be able to guess, and I warn you it'll only be a guess, as to the origin of the bones, animal or human. However, there is another side we haven't even discussed yet." He led the way across the laboratory. The sawdust and bone meal sample had been crammed into a fifty-litre carboy, with a connection at the bottom and the top. Connected to the carboy was a flask and a pump. The contents of the flask were slowly pumped into the carboy top, trickled over the sawdust, and were pumped out at the bottom. In the pumping chain was a sintered glass filter to hold back the fine wet sawdust sludge. The contents of the flask were clear.

"Saline solution," Bradbury explained. "Where you get bones often you get blood. We can identify the blood without question." He switched off the pump, withdrew the stopper from the flask, and collected one cubic centimetre of the liquid in a pipette. He placed the liquid on a flat petrie dish. On the platform of another microscope was a flat plate of glass his assistant had put there, with a drop of liquid on it. Put your eye to the microscope," Bradbury commanded. Aveyard could see the bubble of liquid, perfectly clear. "What you have there," Bradbury explained, is a serum obtained from the blood of rabbits injected with protein from humans. There are two drops." Aveyard cautiously moved the slide until he had the second drop beneath the eye-piece of the microscope. "This liquid," Bradbury said, uncorking a small phial, "is a serum obtained from rabbit blood, but using the protein of felis domesticus, what you would call a common household cat. My own, actually, a ginger tom. He squawked like hell." Bradbury bent forward and deftly dropped one tiny drop of the cat serum into the pool of liquid on the slide. Aveyard had his eye to the eye-piece. He waited. After a minute, he stepped back from the microscope and rubbed his eyes. Bradbury laughed. "Now you know why we all wear glasses," he said. "Did you see anything happen."

Aveyard shook his head. "Not a thing."

Bradbury looked through the microscope, then moved the slide so that the other spot of serum was beneath the lens.

"Watch now," he said. This time, Bradbury took a drop of the solution from the sawdust, added it to the rabbit serum. Aveyard waited, waited. It started in about forty seconds. Suddenly, what had been a clear liquid, was now cross hatched with long needle-like crystals, woven into each other like the strands of shredded wheat. "I can see crystals," he said excitedly.

"Precipitin," Bradbury said. "What you've got in that sawdust, my lad, is human blood!"

There is a device on the front of a tractor allows you to couple on a hydraulic lift, operated from the driving seat when the engine's running. You can put a bucket of three hundredweights capacity on the hydraulic, and still lift it over head height. A metal flange on the lifter arm stops the bucket falling onto the head of the man in the driving seat.

For three consecutive Sunday mornings Cevicec had been filing down the flange; now there was only a sixteenth of an inch left, and a full bucket would certainly jump it.

CHAPTER EIGHT

Saturday afternoon in the village, and villagers prepare for the rigours of self-entertainment. In the twenty-four council houses built in blocks of four at the bottom end of West Lodge Road there are no problems. Sam Gainer, up to his old tricks, has organised a social evening for the kids in the Girl Guide hall by the Green, almost opposite his shop. They'll be there, thirteen to seventeen, dancing to Soul, a word that until recently they've associated with heel. Sam's hoping to start a youth club, but it's uphill all the way. Once they had a youth club until one unaccountable May evening when without warning, youth on a rampage broke all the fittings. "You can't live in the past," Sam says, but memory lingers when folk fork out good money. Seventeen and over they're scattered; some travel to Birton on the bus for the dance at the YMCA, the Tin Hat, or Smiley's Discotheque, admittance two bob and beer in pints. Young marrieds stay home since there's no-one to mind the kids, and the houses aren't big enough to have Mum living in. Older marrieds take a chance, leave the ten to thirteens to look after Willie still in the cot, and spend a social evening sitting on hard chairs at sloppy tables in St Michael's Working Men's Club. There'll be Bingo; Saturday night's the Grand Prize night, a set of glasses, a leatherette shopping bag, a vacuum flask, you never know your luck. The beer was lousy; they've changed the brewery and the price has gone down a half-penny a pint. The beer's still lousy, but the committee dare not admit it, since they voted the move. Give it time to settle! The bungaloids will go to the pictures, or book to eat scampi and boeuf bourguignon at The Pheasant at Marston Ferrers.

An early monopoly game is just finishing in a bungalow on Bent Hill, and Arnold Sudbury is breaking the commandment that says 'thou shalt not fancy thy neighbour's wife!' The kids'll be out soon, Jeanne Sudbury upstairs for her Saturday bath, Walter Nasset next door to hear the news, leaving his wife Virginia for Arnold to bend over the back of the sitting-room couch. It's the only way in tights.

Robin Gotch lives in the cottage at the bottom of Bent Hill almost opposite the Green by the junction with New Farm Road. A carpenter by trade and hobby, he works in Duston making chairs from glued sawdust and bent plywood. At home, he carves the tops of blanket boxes with hand-mortised joints and solid brass handles, tables with fine spindly legs, armoires, inlaid writing boxes, work so delicate and fine he can hardly bear to part with it. He built himself a workshop behind the cottage, a sacrosanct haven with a Yale lock. He doesn't know his son Richard has a key. Saturday night Gotch will be where he is every night, out in his workshop. He's acquired a load of oak from Cattell, virgin wood he can't keep his hands off. At this moment, Gotch is blazing mad; he's just stepped in a pile Richard's spaniel had dropped outside the shed door. "He knows you don't like him, Dad, and that's why he does it there. If only you'd say him a kind word . . ."

"The day I start talking to dogs, you can lock me up . . ."

"I don't mean talk to him; just give him a friendly pat now and then." It's no use; Robin Gotch can't forget his wife, who ran away when the kids were little, always had a bloody poodle hanging about somewhere.

Detective Inspector Aveyard was sitting in the police station with Sergeant Bruton. "Human blood, Jim," he said, "where do we start?"

Jim Bruton sat there, still. He knew the question was rhetorical. But where do you start? Human blood mixed with sawdust beneath a sawbench, and bone bits. Everybody accounted for in the village, except one housewife and her two-year-old daughter. A skeleton found, but that didn't mean a thing since it dated back to the war.

"If Falstaff hadn't found that jawbone, we'd never have been here," he said. It was not a complaint. "We shan't get much sense out of the village this time on a Saturday," he said. "They'll all be going out, or they'll have gone out."

"Our first job, of course, is . . ."

"To find Mrs Holdeness and Christine?"

Aveyard nodded.

"Who could be anywhere," the sergeant added. "London, Blackpool, Brighton."

"Or in Bent?"

"Under the sod?"

Aveyard nodded again. "It'd help," he said, "if we can trace her out of the village. The last we know is that she was in Sam Gainer's getting her forty fags and, let me think, Sam told me who was in before her, single name, now what was it . . ." He picked up the telephone, opened a local directory, found the name he wanted, and dialled the three digits. "Bill here," he said, when Sam Gainer answered. "Remember when you showed me the book with the entry in it for forty fags. Who did you say was in the shop just before?"

"Hang on a minute, I'll look." There was a pause on the line, then Sam's voice came back again. "Fran, that's who it was."

"Fran?"

"Yes, Fran. Lives up in Tolly's with MM."

"MM?"

"Malcolm Minton. We always call him MM, and we always call Fran, Fran. I don't know why." He chuckled. "You going up there to have a word?"

"I thought I might."

"Then I'd better say no more," Sam said, chuckling still. "But don't forget, Cluney wants you back here for supper if you're still going to be in the village."

"I've got a date!"

"Bring her with you. Anybody we know?"

"Local!"

"That'll be Ingeborg. She was just in here buying a shampoo. You must have made an impression. Mind how you go . . ." Sam Gainer hung up the telephone. Aveyard continued holding the instrument to his ear. What had Sam said, "Then I'd better say no more?" Why shouldn't he say any more?

It was a quarter to six when Aveyard walked up the path that led through the copse to Tolly's. The Rectory was up a drive to his right, the Church gaunt beyond it. Several large copper beech trees, elm, oak, a gorgeous spread of conifers. The path bent to the left, up a hill then suddenly turned right along the crest of the hill. The path itself had been surfaced quite recently, and was lined each side with flowering shrubs, deutzia, veronica, azalea. There'd be daffodils in spring, aconites, crocuses, snowdrops. As he broke through the belt of trees, suddenly he saw the house, a low squat stone building of two storeys. Upstairs there were three sets of windows, downstairs two and the door at the side. Tucked to the side and behind the house he could see the ends of other buildings, but whether barns or stables he couldn't tell. In front of the house the macadam swung round in a circle and in the centre was an elevated rose bed. There were flower beds under each of the windows, and a profusion of blooms everywhere. You learn to photograph buildings, to check doors and windows.

A man of about forty was hoeing the rose bed in the centre of the drive. He was dressed in one of those linen jackets you don't see often these days, and on his head he wore a hat in wickerwork pattern of stiffened cotton. His trousers were of the type they sell in the Sunday newspapers as 'ex-Army Officer's Denim'. On his feet he wore hob-nailed boots, an odd touch.

"Good afternoon, Inspector," he said. He put down his hoe, wiped his hands on his trousers, and proffered one as if it were a golden chalice. Aveyard took it, shook it. Despite the heat of the afternoon, it was cold and clammy.

"Everybody seems to know who I am," Aveyard said, in mock complaint.

"That's because you're a *celebrity*. We don't often get *celebrities* in Bent," the man said. There was no suggestion of a lisp in his high-pitched voice. His hair was prematurely silver at the sides. Aveyard glanced at his hands. They were well tended, with clear varnish on the nails. "My name's Malcolm Minton," he said, "but simply everybody calls me MM, so you must, too!"

"Actually, I was looking for Fran," Aveyard said.

"Oh, were you!" MM pouted. "Well, Fran's inside." He went to the door of the house, opened it, called shrilly, "Fran, Fran, police are here, mustn't keep them waiting." Aveyard wondered what sort of a woman could put up with a cissified character such as MM, with his pretty mincing ways. He soon had the answer when the door opened again, and *Fran* came out. Fran was about sixty to sixty-five, Aveyard would guess, and a man. Or at least, what passes for a man in that twilight world. "Dammit," Aveyard thought, "Sam Gainer might have warned me!"

The three of them stood awkwardly together on the driveway, exchanging identities. Fran invited Aveyard inside, MM suggested he'd prefer to stay out of doors. Fran offered him a cup of tea, MM suggested the inspector would surely prefer coffee, or something stronger. Fran offered cigarettes which neither Aveyard nor MM smoked. MM smiled his little triumph, led them across the macadam to the lawn where there was a metal table and four chairs.

"You'd better put a cushion in yours," MM said to Fran, "you don't want to catch a chill!"

MM smiled at Aveyard, complacently. "Fran doesn't look after himself," he said. "I have to think of simply everything. Now, I imagine you want to interrogate us?"

Aveyard laughed; though it sounded a little strained. "Not exactly to 'interrogate' you," he said. "I merely want to ask, er . . ."

"Oh do call him Fran, everyone does!"

". . . to ask Fran a couple of questions." He turned to Fran. "I know it's a few days ago, but can you remember as far back as Tuesday, when you were in the shop?"

"Fran has a poor memory," MM said. "I doubt if he'll remember as far back as that."

Aveyard looked beseechingly at him. Fran cleared his throat. "Yes, I can remember Tuesday. I went to the shop."

"The inspector's just told you that . . ." MM said.

"Could you just let him tell me in his own way?" Aveyard asked.

"You'll be here all night," MM pouted.

"I was in the shop, yes. What is it you want to know?"

"Did you see anyone else in the shop?"

"Anyone else? Sam Gainer, do you mean?"

"No, Fran, the inspector doesn't mean Sam Gainer. He means *anybody else*," MM said, interrupting.

"Would you please just let him tell me in his own way?" Aveyard asked. MM relapsed into silence, sulking.

"Were any other customers in the shop when you got there? Did anyone come in while you were there?" Aveyard asked Fran.

"Virginia Nasset, you know, from the bungalows, she was there when I got there. While Sam was serving me, that Holdeness woman came in, you know, the girl who was Samantha Binns before she married . . ."

"The names they give them," MM simpered.

"You came out of the shop before Mrs Holdeness?"

"Yes."

"Where was the baby, Christine?"

"Outside the shop, in her pram."

"How do you know?"

"Mad about babies, Fran is," MM said, before Fran had a chance to reply, "he can never pass one by."

"I stopped and talked to the baby, why not?"

"Did you wait there until Mrs Holdeness came out?"

"Yes!"

Half a policeman's work is straight question and answer. Recording the facts, or what people think are the facts, on the blueprint of memory. But the other half is, call it what you will, feeling, intuition, extra-sensory perception. Why had Fran suddenly become truculent, talking about the baby? Was it simply his homosexuality, the knowledge he could never have one? Was it simply because he retained some streak of sentimentality he knew MM would deride? What was it? Why was it there, suddenly, as palpable as the silence when a white girl announces she's going to marry a Negro? or a Christian a Jew? Or, for that matter, a Negro a white girl, or a Jew a Christian?

"Did you speak to Mrs Holdeness?"

"Yes, we said a few words to each other."

"Time of the day, how's the weather, that sort of thing?"

Again that palpable silence. Fran looked at MM, troubled.

"Tell the inspector what he wants to know," MM said.

Suddenly, it was as if a curtain had been twitched aside, and Fran had been exposed as no more than a puppet, dangling on strings under MM's control. The waspishness, the affected attitude, this was all a camouflage, Aveyard felt. "Tell the inspector what he wants to know," MM said. It was almost a command.

"She was crying. Talking about leaving her husband. I walked up to the bus-stop with her, and waited with her until I could see the bus coming. I watched her get on the bus."

Bingo! "She took Christine on the bus with her?"

Double Bingo. Now they had an independent witness. The sergeant would be delighted; he revelled in corroboration.

"And the bus left, and that's the last you saw of her?"

"I waited until the bus was out of sight."

Buses into Birton were every hour, a twenty-five-minute run from the bus station to the terminus at Chaldwell, a five-minute wait, twenty-seven minutes back since there was a long hill to climb. Chaldwell, Welby, Bent, Birton, and often the bus arrived full at Bent. The six thirty, however, was almost empty. "Six thirty on a Saturday and the bus almost empty?" Aveyard said, as the conductress took his money. "The five thirty was bulging at the seams," she said, "we turned two off at Bent." Strange, there'd been no-one waiting at the bus stop. "A lot of 'em get lifts," she said, "the bus company doesn't like that; it's loss of revenue, isn't it, I mean, if private cars is picking up passengers."

"You on duty Tuesday?"

"Who wants to know?"

"I do. I'm a police officer."

"Are you, really? Bit young, aren't you?"

"Some of us are teenagers. Were you on duty? How do you work it, on rota?"

"That's right, three on two off. I was off yesterday and the day before, that'd be like Friday and Thursday, so I'd be Wednesday and Tuesday, wouldn't I?"

"Tuesday. What was the seven thirty like? Crowded?"

"Blimey, how can you expect me to remember that?"

"Think about it."

She went upstairs to change the indicator panel. By rights it shouldn't be altered until they got to the bus station, but doing it now would mean extra time in the tea room. He looked at her as she came down the steps. Her brow was furrowed, as if in concentration. "Can't remember anything," she said. "I mean, we do that many trips up and down, out and back, they're all alike, it's the same every time. You get used to it. Sometimes you're full, sometimes you're empty, but unless there's an actual incident, like, I mean there's nothing to stick in your mind, is there?"

"Prams. Do you get many on?"

"Sometimes. *Push chairs*, parcels, suitcases. Nuisance really; some of 'em fill the platform, never a thought we've got to work here?"

"Did you get a *pram* on the bus on Tuesday, the seven thirty? At Bent. Woman, about twenty-eight, wearing a blue coat, baby in the pram aged two . . ."

"That's old to be in a pram . . ."

"This was special."

"Oh aye, one of them mongols, eh?"

"Not exactly."

"I'd 'a noticed if it'd been a mongol. My sister 'ad one, that died when it was one. The doctors ought never to allow 'em to be born, I always say."

They were drawing into the bus station. "Come in," he said, "I'll buy you a cup of tea."

The bus rolled into its bay and the several people on it dismounted. The station had a three-sided services block behind railings; rest rooms, inspector's offices, enquiries and information, a booking office for coach trips to London, a ladies, no gents, but a tea bar. All the walls in sight were painted bottle green to a height of about five feet, cream after that. All high gloss paint, all chipped here and there on the corners. The walls had been washed to about six feet high, arcs where the swabbing woman's arm had reached. He bought the conductress a cup of tea.

"What's your name, then?"

"Aveyard."

"You a sergeant or something?"

"How did you guess?"

"You're serious. The constables are a bit cheeky with it."

"I'm an inspector."

"Blimey, no wonder you're serious. About this bus, the seven thirty on Tuesday, honest, I just can't remember. I've been thinking, but honest, I can't remember a single thing about it. I mean, I know I was on it, and if we look at the ticket sales we'd be able to find out how many people was on it, but I can't remember no pram, nor a girl in a blue coat getting on at Bent. Still, if you say she did get on, I can't deny it, either."

Damnation! It's all so easy in detective stories, isn't it, Aveyard fumed. Perry Mason, Nero Wolfe. "Yes, I saw him, I remember, he was wearing a gold signet ring with the badge of The Royal Army Ordnance Corps!" But it doesn't happen like that in real life. Where was your Aunt Fanny on the night of the seventeenth? Who the hell knows? Who can remember, when you ask 'em. Grey faces passing over the platform of a bus, hands holding coins, muted voices that name sums of money or destinations to which you give them tickets. You never look at the faces, and if you do, they all vanish rapidly into a grey curtain of mutual indifference. Sometimes a lad gets on, good looking, but your hormones recall him, not your memory. Sometimes an old bag gets on with a mountain of string bags and says "you're late." You look at her and think, "Yes, you old bag, and I'd like to stick that hat pin just where it'd do you the most good"; but hate suppresses memory as often as it recalls it.

"There's no charge for prams, is there?"

"None at all. I believe there's supposed to be, like there is for dogs, but we never ask for it. You was hoping there might be a special ticket issued? Well, if I had charged, it'd be just like any other ticket."

"Can you remember any one, any single person, on that bus?" Long slow job. The sergeant, and his band of merry men. Find someone, any one who travelled on that bus. Notices in the buses. 'Would any person who travelled on the seven thirty bus to Birton on the night of Tuesday please communicate with . . .' You'll be lucky. Involve myself with the police. Not on your nellie! Go round the villages on route. Only three hundred or thereabouts in Welby. Door to door. Did you travel on the bus? But then, if you're exceedingly lucky and you find even one person, will they remember, a woman in a blue coat, and a pram. They might, they just might.

Anyway, it'd give the sergeant something to do. That's the sort of enquiry Jim Bruton revels in, with his slow methodical mind. He'd draw up a chart or two, get out his coloured ball point pens. Bill Aveyard gave him a pack of twelve of each colour for Christmas last year. It was meant as a giggle, nothing more. But Bruton was so grateful. "You couldn't have picked anything I'd rather have . . ."

"I've got to go now," she said.

"Hang on, I'm coming with you."

"You got an idea?"

"No, I've got a date."

"Cheeky," she said, "and you an inspector!"

Walter Nasset lived in the bungalows with his wife and two cats. Virginia Nasset was changing, since they expected guests. Walter came out of the bathroom clad only in a towel. He'd shaved, rubbed his chin with cologne brought back from Sardinia, and combed his silvery hair. Virginia was wearing pants and nothing else, sitting at a sapele dressing table, making up her eyes. "On the films," he said, "I'd sneak up behind you, put my arms about you, and draw you back onto the bed."

"Too bad you're not on the films!"

He walked across the carpet, put his arms about her, cupping her breasts. He rubbed his chin on her hair; his fingers moved over her breasts. She sat there, looking in the mirror. Love grows old and waxes cold and fades like summer's dew. She reached behind her, her hand twitching the towel aside. Nothing, absolutely nothing.

"Too bad I'm not a boy scout," she said.

CHAPTER NINE

"I didn't think you'd turn up," Ingeborg said, when she answered the door. He followed her inside the cottage. Stone built, with what the estate agents hopefully call, a wealth of exposed beams. Walls of wattle, uneven, emulsion painted in magnolia. A home, not a house.

"Is there any reason I shouldn't have come?"

"Don't be coy," she said. Horst Cattell acknowledged his arrival with a friendly grunt, then went back to his library book. Flemming leaped up, smiling as ever. "Have this chair," he said, "it's comfortable." Supper pots had been cleared away, the place was neat and tidy. Horst wearing his slippers, and a pair of spectacles. He'd changed out of his working clothes but whether in honour of Aveyard or Saturday night, it'd be hard to tell. Flemming was wearing a tie, had slicked down his hair, long in the modern style. He was wearing hipster trousers, a striped coloured shirt, and a green suede leather tie. He looked fine! His boots were almost yellow!

"That's the book I was reading," she said, indicating a copy of *Royal Flash* by her chair, "if you really want to read over my shoulder; or I could even find you a book for yourself!"

"We've got an invitation."

"I know," she said, "but that's up to you."

"How do you know?"

"Questions, questions. I had to go back to the shop, that's how I know, and Sam said, I understand we may be seeing you. At the time, he was wearing a green sweater over beige trousers, holding a yellow pencil in his left hand, a red book in his right hand, and there was a distinct smudge of black coal dust down the side of his flesh-coloured nose. The left side!" They both laughed. "Pity you're not a bus conductor," Aveyard said, "but, don't let's get on to that subject."

"Are we dining out?"

"Cluney's a good cook."

"That settles it," she said, "I'm strictly bacon and eggs." She put on a light coat and they left. Simple as that. No make-up. He thought with wry amusement of the number of times he had waited for a girl to run a comb through her hair, the number of half hours wasted. "Don't be late," her father said, a homely touch, not an injunction.

It was a warm evening, almost close. "Don't get much breeze here," she said. "I think it must be all the trees." She slipped her hand through his arm. "Villages are very enclosed places," she said; "it's nice to have somebody new . . ."

"Sam Gainer and Cluney are new."

"That's it," she said, "Sam Gainer *and* Cluney. Now, if he was single, I might snap him up!"

The path from the cottage came into the top of New Farm Road. They turned left down the slope. New Farm Road's straight and ends at the pub on the Green at what's called Five Lane Ends. Bent Road and Bent Hill on the left, Sam Gainer's shop and post-office at the corner. Next door to Sam Gainer's was Phil Wilkins' butcher shop, and behind it the house where he lives with his kids, Josie, Fred and Bob. He couldn't make a living out of Bent, had a contract to supply pie-meat to a Birton pie-maker 'fresh every day', and sausages to the canteen of a large shoe factory in Chaldwell. With three hundred and fifty employees it was lucrative business. Sausages were always on, either for dinner or tea, supper for the night shift. "They say he makes a good sausage," Ingeborg said, "but I only tasted them once and found too much pepper for my taste. His father was known throughout the county."

As they waited to cross Bent Road, a large transporter came down Bent Hill from the Birton Road, turned across Bent Road, and pulled in behind the butcher's. The driver of the van reversed, so that the back of the van was flush with the building. There was a splash of light as the door into the back of the shop was opened; it was impossible to see into the shop because of the van. "Bit late to be delivering meat?" Aveyard said.

"He's on the go all the time," she said. "He must be making a mint of money."

A warm evening in June, walking along a road with a new girl, height of adventure. Side by side, companionable talk without restraint. She told him the name of the occupants of each cottage they passed, a quick verbal sketch of the inhabitants, a Cook's Tour of Bent. She was obviously far more intelligent than her work in the wood yard would suggest. He told her so. "You've seen Fleming," she said. "He'd make a mess of the business, and one day it'll come to him. I'm just trying to keep everything on an even keel for him."

"But what about your own interests?"

"I have them, too," she said, "the one thing doesn't interfere with the other."

"You haven't thought of getting married, yet?"

"I've thought about it, haven't you, haven't we all?" she said, "but I'm just not certain about the marriage thing. I don't go for drugs, protest marches, the Civil Liberties bit, but a lot of things are changing. You'd be surprised, even in these dull backwaters, how much we keep in touch with what's going on. It seems to me two of our institutions need redefining. One's the Church, and the other's marriage. I want to know a bit more about myself before I make any decisions," she said. "I'm suspending judgment!" They were standing outside the shop.

"About the bone dust," he said. He touched her arm. She turned to look at him and he held her arm, gently.

"We could do the same with that, if you wanted?" she said.

"Suspend judgment?"

"If you want to?"

"I do."

"Then I'd better call you Bill," she said, "and not Inspector!" Cluney and Sam were waiting for them, and Cluney had prepared a supper of home-made paté, an open ham and egg pie, and soufflé. There was a choice of cheeses, and coffee. The men drank a sixty-six Beaujolais Sam Gainer bought by the case in Birton, Ingeborg and Cluney a Piesporter. When Cluney had cleared the table and she and Ingeborg were in the kitchen, washing up, Sam got out a bottle of Irish whiskey, two glasses, a jug of water.

"Do you think they'd mind?" he asked, indicating the chess board.

"Why don't you have a game of chess, you two," Cluney shouted from the kitchen.

"She's psychic," Sam explained as gleefully he set up the pieces. By tacit agreement no-one mentioned police business.

They left shortly after eleven o'clock to walk back through the village together. Somehow, it seemed natural to hold hands. "How marvellous that you should know Sam and Cluney," Ingeborg said. "When they bought the post-office, they brought a breath of fresh air into Bent."

There are three cottages at the bottom of Bent Hill. From the back of the first they could hear Robin Gotch planing wood, the rhythmic precision of a craftsman. No-one was about, the moon was already high above the trees. The second cottage was entirely dark, the third cottage had lights downstairs and up. Beyond the third cottage was Doug Minsell's New Farm. The ghostly figures of horses came across the paddock, stood at the hedge, hoping.

"I should have brought them a cube of sugar," Aveyard said.

"It's bad for their teeth!"

They came to the hump of the bridge over the stream that runs through Bent. He stood on the bridge, looking over the parapet, down into the trickle of water. The stream was six feet wide at the most, but tinkled delightfully. She looked over the parapet with him. He half turned his face towards her, was conscious of her face, half turned towards him. There's a moment of decision at each stage of a relationship between people. So far they'd met, been attracted. So far they were acquaintances. Hand holding when they left Sam Gainer's had made them friends. What would they become if he were to answer his unspoken desire, her silent invitation, and kiss her? There's a danger in becoming lovers, since lovers can rarely be friends again. The water glistened; the shadows of their heads, cast by the moon behind them, changing shape on the surface of the rippling water, drew nearer. Neither spoke, listening to the music of the stream, the muted strains of their tentative feelings for each other. Aveyard turned his head, found hers already turned towards him, and kissed her awkwardly on the lips. He was holding her hand, made no attempt to put his other hand about her. His eyes were open. Hers had closed, then opened again as the kiss continued. She pressed his hand, then drew her lips back from his. Their faces were close together.

"Hello," she said, softly.

"Hello." He turned his head away, looked over the parapet again, his thoughts racing, anxious to stem desire, to hold it in check.

And then he saw the body, half in, half out of the stream. He vaulted the parapet, landed on the bank of the stream below. The body was lying face down. He turned it over. The head lolled, neck broken. Aveyard scrambled up the bank, burst his way through a small gap in the hedge.

"Wait here," he said, "do you mind?"

"Who is it, is he dead?"

"That boy Holdeness. Looks as if his neck's broken."

"You'd be in trouble if anyone found out. I might tell, you know!"

He looked at her, his hatred ill-concealed. Her expression softened as she looked at him. "I shan't tell anybody, as long as we can go on meeting."

"We're meeting now, aren't we?"

"Yes, but I had to threaten you to get you to come out."

"It's damned dangerous meeting at this time of night. One of these days, you'll go too far threatening me."

She reached up and pulled a handful of the deadly nightshade leaves. "I could eat that!"

"It's the berries that are poison, and they don't come out until October, more's the pity."

"By then," she said, "you could be a daddy all over again!"

CHAPTER TEN

The pathologist grumbled, but no-one took him seriously. It was unusual for him to get on to a job so early; often hours elapsed before he was called in but this time, as he confirmed within minutes of his arrival, the body had been dead only about forty-five minutes. Five minutes for Aveyard to belt up the hill to the police station telephone, five minutes for them to find the pathologist in a dinner party in the Chaldwell House Hotel, fifteen minutes for him to get to the bridge, five minutes for him to examine the body where it lay, on the bank of the stream. Death must have occurred only fifteen minutes before Aveyard saw the body. "That must be some kind of record," the pathologist said to Aveyard, "but I do wish you chaps would remember not to move the body!"

"He was half in half out of the water. I didn't know he was dead. It was natural to get him up on the bank."

"You chaps don't seem to understand; we can tell an awful lot from the exact position of the body. Did he fall over the bridge, was he drunk, did he land on his head, was he pushed? You've three things to go for, Inspector, accidental death, suicide, or murder, and it would have helped me help you if I'd been able to study the exact lie of the body . . . That's all we're trying to do, you know, to help you!" Aveyard squirmed under the lecture.

"You forgot one other possibility," he said. Try this one for size. "Manslaughter. Two men having a giggle on the bridge, or a man and a girl, she gives him a gentle push, and over he goes. She gets scared, runs away. You'd never get a conviction for murder. It'd be damned hard even to get one for manslaughter."

The pathologist didn't like being lectured, either. "You finished?" he asked the photographers, testy. They nodded. "Right," he said to the men from the forensic laboratory. "You can take him. I'll pick up Dr Samson, and we'll start an autopsy a bit later on."

"When will that be, sir?" the forensic sergeant asked.

"How do I know, sergeant; it'll depend on when I can get hold of Dr Samson." Aveyard had rattled him, smiling smugly. The forensic men lifted the body on to a polythene sheet, then four of them took the corners and hoisted the body up on to the roadway. They'd brought an old police ambulance with them that sometimes did duty as a Black Maria; out came the ubiquitous box, the polythene bundle was carefully lowered into it, and the ambulance was driven away. The photographers packed up their equipment, and they too drove away. The pathologist sniffed, barked a cursory good night to Aveyard, and left in search of Dr Samson. For him the night would be spent examining every facet of the corpse of Humphrey Holdeness; he had reason to be out of humour. Ingeborg had gone home when the squad had arrived. That left Aveyard, Bruton, Sergeant Manners, Constable Verney, and four of Aveyard's men from Birton. "I'll take Binns and the pub," Aveyard said. Sergeant Bruton nodded. "I could use two extra hands," he said to Sergeant Manners, regretting he'd let the search party go after breakfast. Manners looked at Joe Verney. Neither was a detective, neither had the training or experience to be able to handle the specialised work, but presumably Bruton knew what he was doing. It was a volunteer job, of course. Once Birton had been called in, strictly speaking it was their pigeon. "I could give you a couple of hours," he said, "and maybe Joe here isn't in a hurry to get to bed?" Joe nodded, though reluctantly. "Thank you. I want every house covered, starting at the Birton road at the bottom, coming all the way up Bent Hill. My lads know the form, what time did you come in, did you see anything in the road, have you seen Holdeness etc etc. If you could go with my lads and introduce them at the doors, it'll save that much time." A lot of valuable minutes can be lost establishing bona fides on the doorstep. The Birton men were plain clothes, Sergeant Manners and Joe Verney were both uniformed, and known to the villagers.

Arthur Binns was sitting in his chair, fully dressed, in the room behind the pub; John Scotia, who ran the pub for him and hoped one day to take it over, was washing glasses at the sink in the bar. Joanna Spraggs, who lived in the next council house to the Holdeness family, and helped out in the bar on Saturdays, had gone home. She'd be back in the morning to sweep up, stack the glasses John had washed. He paid her fifteen bob for helping Saturdays; she'd have done it free of charge to be near him. She too had aspirations she was hoarding for when Arthur Binns gave it up.

"What can you tell me about your son-in-law's parents, Mr Binns," Aveyard asked, after he had broken the news of the death.

"He had none, at least, none as anybody knew about."

"Orphanage?"

"That's right, in Chaldwell. I told him many a time he ought to try and trace his parents, but it seemed like he just didn't care to re-open old sores. But I told him, you can't go on holding a grudge all your life, and whoever they are, somewhere they might be lonely in their old age and in need of a son's love. But I couldn't shift him. All for hisself, that's what he was, all for hisself. I was agin it, the wedding, I mean. I reckon she threw herself away, our Samantha did, and her that was brought up right from the day she was born. Course, it put paid to her up there, my Nell. Never been the same, she hasn't, since the wedding."

"When was the last time you saw your son-in-law, Mr Binns?"

"The last time I pulled a pint in that bar. He never come in here. He'd come in the pub, mark you, stand there supping all night, but never come in here to pass the time of day, and his mother-in-law's life just slipping away."

"Was he in the pub tonight?"

"How should I know, I never go in there."

"I just thought John Scotia might have mentioned it?"

"More to do he has than standing here gossiping about who's in the bar and who isn't."

"I shall be having a word with him in a minute; he can tell me, but I just thought you might know?"

A copper's nose is better than that of a pointer, and though a fact may be a fact, it's the way a fact's presented that often gives it significance. Aveyard suspected the old man knew everything that went on in the pub.

"Well, as a matter of fact, now you come to mention it, he was in here tonight. John did just happen to mention it."

"Buy a lot of beer?"

"What, him? Too bloody mean to lash out. He had his usual four pints and a packet of crisps, and he bought himself twenty tipped Weights."

So, the old bugger did know what was going on. "Did he do much talking usually?"

"Not a lot. He had a game of darts wi' Laszlo . . ."

"Laszlo?" Aveyard interrupted.

"Laszlo Cevicec, the poor sod whose wife our Humphrey was knocking on the sly."

"They played darts? Often?"

"Whenever they were in the place together. That's how Laszlo got his revenge; he always beat our lad rotten at darts."

"So Cevicec knew your son-in-law was seeing his wife?"

"Course he knew."

"He didn't mind?"

"Why should he. Humphrey wasn't the first, take my word for that, and every time some other bugger did her, that made one time less that Laszlo had to, didn't it?" The old man chuckled. What did he mean, 'take my word for that'? Had he been one of the 'other buggers' who'd 'done' her?

Old men left alone to brood have fertile imaginations, strange fantasies. Hidden desires grow malignant, old slights fester like sores. "One of your old girl friends, was she?" Aveyard asked, pretending a conspiratorial chuckle. "Me, I wouldn't touch her with a barge-pole!" Too much indignity, old man, too vehement. You had tried to touch her, hadn't you, and not with a barge-pole. And now, get off the subject quickly. You'll get no more truth on that one.

"What time did Cevicec leave?"

"Laszlo? He's never late. He'd be out of here by closing time."

"Half past ten?"

"On the dot, you don't catch us staying open late and jeopardising the licence." Lying sod—ten to one he got the phrase from a policeman's warning!

"And Humphrey, what time did he go?"

"Early tonight. He left about ten o'clock. Most unusual for him."

The word 'unusual' rings a bell for an investigating

officer every time it sounds. 'Unusual' events lead to crime, 'unusual' movements expose criminals. Holdeness left early tonight. The next question would be 'why?' But this was not the time or place to ask it.

In the police station, Jim Bruton had assembled one of his time and place charts covering the relevant part of the evening. Routine, but Bruton's speciality. Let the inspector indulge in flights of fancy, investigate motives. Sooner or later, he'd have to come to Bruton for the physical facts of movement.

"Sam Gainer's dance in the Village Hall didn't break up until eleven thirty and they were all having such a good time nobody left; so you can rule that lot out. A certain police officer who shall be nameless was seen proceeding up Bent Hill in company with a young lady from the village. According to my reports, they appeared to be holding hands . . ."

"Cheeky sod, get on with your report."

"They were seen, kissing! Then, the police officer appeared to be so excited, he jumped over the parapet of the bridge into the water. Presumably to cool himself off!"

"That's interesting!"

"I thought it would be. It means, of course, that somebody could see that bridge, since I presume that's where the alleged kiss took place?" Sergeant Bruton was keeping a straight face with difficulty. Aveyard smiled at him, raised his head in a superior fashion. "Now I ask you, Jim, if you'd been with a girl like that, on a night like this, in a place like that, what would you have done?"

"I'd have had a quick look round to make certain I couldn't be seen. But then, in my generation, we weren't so bold. Still, it means we know the bridge was under observation, and that's something. Unfortunately, although two separate people report seeing you kiss, nobody was looking out of the windows earlier on. Nobody can report seeing Holdeness there."

"Where was Mary Cevicec? Say, at ten o'clock?"

Bruton turned his papers. "Ten o'clock, Mary Cevicec would be on her way back home."

"Where from?"

"That's the funny thing. She said she'd been for a walk. She slipped out of the house at nine o'clock, walked up West Lodge Road, turned into Grove Gardens. Destination was the Village Hall by the Green. Two of her kids, Heather and Roger, were at the dance. Apparently it was an experiment tonight, because Sam Gainer usually puts the records on for them. Tonight they had made up a group from the village, and they were nervous of playing in front of any adults, and so Sam said they could get on with it. Annie Spraggs, who apparently is a very sensible lass, was put more or less in charge, but Mary Cevicec didn't entirely trust her. She was afraid that without supervision, the kids might be running some kind of an orgy, I suppose."

"And were they?"

"Apparently not. She came out of there just after nine, and then, to quote her own words, 'it was such a lovely night I decided on the spur of the moment to go for a walk'."

"Route?"

"Grove Gardens, up West Lodge Road, turn right into Church Row, and back to the Green by Bent Hill."

"So, at ten o'clock, she'd be where?"

"My guess would be on the bridge," Bruton said, "anyway, she'd be somewhere near there, coming down Bent Hill."

"Holdeness left the pub at ten, and was later found on that bridge, or rather underneath it. They *must* have met, they *must* have."

"She says they didn't. She says she never saw him. Oh we've got a list from her of the people she did meet, all confirmed. But no Holdeness."

Aveyard walked to the wall, stared at the map of Bent pinned there. "Which way did she go round the Green?"

Jim Bruton came to the map, stood beside the inspector. He had no need to refer to his notes. "She says she came this way, past the War Memorial, crossed New Farm Road end . . ."

"So that'd put her right outside the pub?"

"That's right."

"She *must have met him* . . ."

"She says not . . ."

"Where did she go after the pub?"

"She kept on Bent Hill, all the way to the Birton Road, walked along the Birton Road, here, turned back into West Lodge Road."

"Anybody see her along the Birton Road?"

"No. That's the blind spot. Nobody saw her after the bridge on Bent Hill."

"Aha, aha." Aveyard was triumphant. "Doesn't that strike you as strange that she had complete verification of her story all the way round the village, but not a single witness for the last half of the walk? Doesn't that strike you as 'unusual'?"

"At this stage of the game, Inspector, I'm looking out for facts, only facts. I'll leave all the 'unusual' stuff to you!"

"Right, let's leave the subject of Mary Cevicec. Who saw Holdeness. We know he left the pub at ten o'clock, and that was 'unusual'. But where did he go?"

"Another complete blank."

"You've checked all the window watchers. No, forget I asked that; you've checked them all right or you wouldn't have a report of my kissing! But nobody, absolutely nobody, saw Holdeness?"

"Nobody. Cheryl Minsell was in the field—apparently she often goes to say goodnight to the horses, and she saw Mary Cevicec at the top of Bent Hill, by Church Row. She waved goodnight, Mary Cevicec waved back, but she didn't see Holdeness. Arnold Sudbury had been to the pub for a packet of cigarettes about five past ten, but he didn't see either Cevicec or Holdeness."

"That accounts for the bottom part of Bent Hill. What about Grove Gardens."

Sergeant Bruton referred to his notes. "At five past ten," he said, "Joe Scotia drove his car all the way along Grove Gardens, round the south side of the Green, and down Bent Road to his farmhouse. He saw neither Holdeness nor Mary Cevicec."

"So, at five past ten, we have three people covering the roads that lead from the pub, we know Holdeness left the pub a few minutes before, yet not one of those three people saw him?"

"That's right, and only one of them saw Mary Cevicec."

"Verney gone to bed?"

"I think so."

"Sergeant Manners gone?"

"An hour ago . . ."

Aveyard picked up the telephone and dialled. The sergeant could hear the telephone ringing at the other end. Then there was a clatter as the receiver was knocked off its cradle, the sound of heavy night-time breathing, then, "Gainer, yes, who is it?"

"Bill Aveyard. Sam, I'm sorry to waken you . . ."

"You haven't woken me, I'm still asleep. Give me a half a minute." There was a sound of drinking; when Sam Gainer came back on the line he was fully awake. "What's the matter, Bill?"

He knew about the death of Holdeness, since he was one

of the men who had been questioned. "How well do you know the village, Sam?"

"They all come in the shop, you know."

"Where's the local courting spot. If you had a date with a girl and nowhere to take her, where would you go?"

"I wouldn't be so daft at my time of life, but I'll take the 'you' to mean 'one'. Courting spots, eh? We know one lad had the key to the back door of the Village Hall. That cost him his bachelordom; he got the girl pregnant."

"Not the Village Hall. That was in use at the time I'm interested in." Sam Gainer thought a while, then chuckled. "They use the woods at the back of the police station," he said.

"Cheeky monkeys."

"How about the woods on West Lodge Hill?"

"No, that's not possible. Somewhere near the Green."

"Well, that's dead simple. By the lake inside the grounds of the Hall." Suddenly Aveyard remembered the rhododendron bushes. "That's it," he said, "that could be it. How do you get in there?"

"Dead easy," Sam said, "walk up Bent Hill to the bridge, over the low wall on the left of the road, down the bank, and you're in the grounds of the Hall and lost to sight."

"And the rhododendron bushes about twenty yards ahead?"

"Yes, but if you keep to the left, you're completely hidden by the trees. One or two of 'em used to duck out the back door of the Village Hall, during the dances. We had to put a special lock on it."

"Go back to sleep, Sam, and thank you!"

"Always ready to help," said Sam.

They found the foot-prints by the light of Bruton's torch, but it would be impossible to say which were which.

Certainly the path at the edge of the bridge had been well used. There were the prints of girls' shoes, too, and one set of stiletto heels.

"Thought they went out of fashion years ago," Bruton said.

Aveyard stood by the bridge; it was a warm night though it would grow cold later, just before dawn. There were several lights in the upstairs windows of houses they could see. "I thought these villages were early to bed?" Aveyard said to the sergeant. "Now let's reconstruct. Mrs Cevicec packs her kids off to Sam Gainer's dance, and then at nine o'clock she goes out to make sure they're all right. Nice evening so she takes a walk round the village. She's got a date with her boy-friend at ten o'clock, by the bridge . . ."

"Since her husband's at the pub and the kids are all out, why doesn't she invite him home?" the sergeant asked.

"Home, to a council house, neighbours both sides? They may have been brazen, but that'd be carrying it too far. No, she has a date by the bridge. Holdeness leaves the pub at ten o'clock, and that's unusual for him."

"But since his wife's away, why doesn't he invite her to his house, on some sort of pretext? She could bring a sweeping brush with her, pretend she was going to clean up for him?"

"No, I don't think they'd do that; I don't think they'd run the risk of advertising. Now, Holdeness comes out of the pub, walks up Bent Hill."

"Nobody sees him?"

"Apparently not, and that's just our bad luck. When he gets to the bridge he waits. Perhaps he sees Cheryl Minsell coming across the field, on her way to say goodnight to her horse. Anyway, he ducks down here out of sight. Mary Cevicec comes down the road, he gives her a whistle, and she scrambles down that path. They make their way into the bushes, and spend a half an hour together."

"That means she'll be late home. and what's she going to say to her husband?"

"She's going to tell him she's been looking out for the kids in the Village Hall. Don't forget she's been there once, and she can give an account of who's there and what they're doing."

"She wasn't at home when Cevicec got there, so we know she must have spent time somewhere."

"And she says she was out walking and had no idea what time it was?" Bruton nodded. "Right, they've had their bit of nooky, and they come out of the rhododendrons. They go up on to the bridge, stand there talking. A bit of love play, perhaps, a bit of horseplay, and Holdeness goes over the edge. She looks down, sees him lying still, dead. So she belts home as fast as she can, to divert suspicion. She gives us an accurate account of the early part of her walk because she knows people have seen her. She's telling us the truth, but not all of it."

"What we need is somebody who's seen her, after half past ten, hurrying home."

"And so far you've found no-one?"

"No-one."

Both were silent.

"We can't do any good here tonight," Aveyard said, "you may as well get home and have a night's sleep!"

"What about you, Inspector?"

"I'm not tired. I think I'll walk about a bit, clear my thoughts, and grab a kip in Verney's cell."

"I'll go off on one condition, Inspector." Dead formal, eh?

"And what's that?"

"You promise to get some sleep!"

Aveyard smiled. "You're an old woman, Jim," he said, "but I promise!"

The car waiting outside the police station took Bruton

home. Though his wife was in bed when he arrived, she heard the car draw up at the gate and by the time he got inside the house, she already had the water on for a cup of tea.

"Rhododendron bushes, eh?" he said, looking at his wife in her dressing jacket and night gown. He hugged her to him, she smelt warm, cuddly. "Some people want their heads examining," he said.

Aveyard couldn't sleep, was sitting in the police station, casting his thoughts like flies over the seeming quiet pool of the village life. The surface was still, calm, deceptive; beneath it he knew the roots were slimy and tangled. When the telephone rang he couldn't recognise the sound for a moment, so intense had been his thoughts. Eventually he realised what it was and lifted the receiver.

"Inspector Aveyard?" the voice asked.

"Yes? Speaking!"

"Willie Baines, sir." A constable on the detective squad, newly joined from police college.

"Yes, lad?"

"I had an idea, Inspector, about that bus. Thought I'd check it, see if it came to anything. I think I may have something. Anybody who goes in on the bus probably also comes out on the bus. I've been down in the bus station, checking the buses as they go out, checking all the passengers, I mean."

"Good lad. Good thinking. Any luck?"

"I think so, Inspector. Of course, I was put off because I checked them all this evening, right up to the last scheduled one, without anything. I was just leaving . . ." Aveyard stemmed his impatience; it takes a trained man of a lot of experience to give a short report; young ones are scared of leaving something out. ". . . the bus station when the inspector, I mean the bus inspector, told me there was always an extra on Saturday nights. A young lad on it helped a woman on to a bus at Bent, Tuesday night. She had a pram with her, and he gave her a lift up the step with it, that's how he remembers."

"Description?"

It fitted Samantha Holdeness perfectly. Apparently, she sat on the bus, crying all the way into Birton. The lad felt bothered at not being able to help.

"Did he see where she went?"

"Yes, Inspector. He appears to have his heart in the right place. Of course a lot of people say the younger generation doesn't care . . ." Patience, Bill, patience. ". . . but they do. He helped her off the bus with the pram, walked with her across to the London coach, and saw her on to it. The coach wasn't leaving for ten minutes or so, and he took her over to the buffet and bought her a cup of tea. I remembered what you said about the cigarettes at the briefing, and he said she offered him a cigarette, from a twenty packet, Inspector, from a *twenty* packet, Inspector, from a *twenty* packet . . . !"

"Good lad, Baines." The constable went on to describe the scene as best he could, amplifying his remarks about the younger generation, flattered by having the ear of an inspector into which to spill his theories; the inspector was thinking of other things, troubled, and let him ramble on. Finally, the penny dropped, or whatever happens when your conscious drags the fears of the subconscious into the realms of knowledge.

"One thing you're forgetting, lad," he said, not unkindly. "You haven't said a single word about that baby! You've talked about the pram, but you haven't talked about the baby. Didn't your lad mention it? He put her on a bus, took her off and over to the buffet for a cup of tea, she offered him a fag from a packet of twenty, but where,

where. was. the. baby?"

Baines said, "I'd assumed the baby was in the pram, asleep?"

"All that time? Anyway, whenever did you see a woman leave a baby in a *pram* on a bus platform, even if the baby was asleep? It's against the rules. The *pram* has to be folded, the baby carried inside the bus."

"I don't know, Inspector, I, I haven't had much experience of babies . . ."

"I know you haven't. Don't mind me barking at you. I've had a long day. Where's your informant now? Ask him about the baby."

There was a pause, a silence. "I can't, Inspector," he said. "It was a special bus, you see. They'd held it up for me as it was! I let him go home on it!"

"Good God lad, you could have sent him home in a police car and he'd have been glad of the ride. I'd have authorised it. Anyway, get yourself a car from the pool, and get out to where he lives as fast as you can, and ask him about the baby."

There was another pause.

"You *do* know where he lives?" Aveyard asked, quietly.

"I'm sorry, Inspector, I'm dreadfully sorry. The bus driver was in such a rush, you see, and a lot of the passengers had had quite a bit to drink and there was an uproar, you see, and so I let him jump on and go. I thought I had everything."

There was ice in Aveyard's voice. "What's his name, lad?"

"I meant to fill in his name and address when I'd finished questioning him."

"Baines, listen carefully. I want to know who that lad is, and where he lives. I want him put in a police car and brought here to me. I don't care how you do it, I don't care when, but if you so much as close your eyes before I've had a chance to talk to him, I'll see that you get attached to my sergeant, Bruton, you know him, and he'll have you interviewing deaf and dumb Pakistanis and filling in report forms the correct way until the day he retires. Is that quite clearly understood?"

There was a strangled "Yes!" from the other end of the telephone. Aveyard hung up.

After Baines Aveyard couldn't sleep, couldn't stand the confinement of the police station. He went out and walked along Church Row to the top of New Farm Road. The wood-yard was on his right, massed trunks of once stately trees, felled in their prime, hardening, maturing in death for man to use. Night sounds in the quiet village, peace, hope and despair. Washing hanging on pieces of cord, dimly seen at the sides of cottages, tattered slips, darned under-vests, socks with holes in them. Nothing's new, everything has seen service, known affectionate possession. 'Throw that shirt away, Henry!' 'No, it's comfortable'. 'Here, Mum, me vest's got a hole in it!' 'How the blazes did you get a hole in your vest? Give it here, and I'll mend it some-time!' Sometime can be a long time coming. There are beans to pluck, peas to get out of their pods, potatoes to dig and peel, rabbits to skin, furniture to polish, windows to wash, paths to sweep, beds to make, meals to cook, buns to bake and, if you're lucky, a dab of lipstick and away to the W.I. This week they're going to look round a leather tannery in Irchester, it'll be interesting and the coach is ordered for two. There'll be a bit of a sing-song, and tea with buns after. Virginia Nasset runs it, with Jeanne Sud-bury. Newcomers to the village, of course, bought a bunga-low, and laid a lawn from turf not seed, and that if nothing else marks them out as something special. They've both got their own cars, quite separate from their husbands' cars, they do Meals on Wheels three times a week, the Hospital Transport Service as required, and powder the corrosions of middle-class boredom. They don't belong in Bent, never will. Bent folk are never bored, Bent folk have a consuming interest in the lives of the folk of Bent, and can never therefore be bored. Sarah Minsell's got a new hat, all right for a farmer's wife, isn't it, when she can keep the egg money for herself. That bit of Bent news will occupy twenty minutes of shop waiting time. Hector Spraggs has hurt his ankle and he'll be off work for at least two weeks; that's a Bent item, and Nellie Binns, is she dead yet? they long to ask but the words couldn't come out. There's no cruelty in Bent. "It's marvellous the way she manages to hang on," they'd say. Formula words the dough of local bread. But now a policeman, lots of policemen among them. Joe Verney doesn't count, he's as Bent as the rest. But this inspector, what's his name, Graveyard, what sort of a name is that, oh, Aveyard, sorry!

Night-time walking, the trees sigh. How many are there in Bent, ten thousand? Who counted them? Tall trees stately, squat trees that weep over the stone walls. Once all of Bent belonged to a Bent, now tenant farmers pay the rent to a solicitor in Birton for the benefit of the Estate; it's been a long time since a Bent foot walked these fields, and the ground belongs, by moral if not legal right, to those who beat the bounds. An owl somewhere in the Churchyard makes the only sound. A cat slinks across a road, looking for sex, ashamed. The lights are out in the dwellings, early to bed, early to rise, and few dreams. They ought to dream more, but dreaming's an expansive thing, and Bent drawn in upon itself clings to well-worn reality. A warm night, yes indeed; the smell of hedge blossoms among people who name them in conversation, not to flower speech. A pair of eyes looked out at Aveyard, walking down the road. Alien feet, a foreigner's feet. Everybody who walks down this road touches the edge of the wall by New Farm. Once there was a tragedy by that wall, when a bull got among six who were carting barley. Three died, two gored, one jumped clear over the wall though it's six feet high. It's a local tale they tell, and everybody who walks past touches the wall in remembrance. All except the foreigners. They don't know the story. By these things ye know them. All the men in Bent wear boots Brian King brings home cheap but legal; Aveyard, no man of Bent, wore shoes.

"What the devil are you doing, out at this time of night," Aveyard said to himself in the dark. An accidental death's a sergeant's job at first, and there never was a clearer case. Bones dug up, woman and child missing, small matters when there's a county full of hot crime, violent town crime of greed and avarice, robbery, murder, manslaughter, blackmail, arson, rape and suicide.

A pair of eyes watched Aveyard turn the corner by the wood-yard, watched him walk down the road, deep in thought. A pair of feet started to follow his feet when he had passed, treading silent in the night. Aveyard walked down New Farm Road to the pub at the bottom, turned up Bent Hill And now, another pair of eyes were watching him, watching the person who followed him.

Richard Gotch held his spaniel in his arms, sitting by the window, looking out. Richard Gotch had seen Aveyard before, that evening. He'd held the spaniel in his arms, looking out of the window, saw Aveyard pass with Ingeborg Cattell. He saw them, walking hand in hand, up the street. He saw them walk up holding hands. He hugged his spaniel. Richard Gotch was seventeen, Ingeborg twenty-five, a lifetime away. Now he saw Aveyard again, this time walking on his own, but being followed. He came from the window, tears in his eyes.

"Now don't you dare bark," he said to the spaniel as he

put it on the strip of carpet at the bottom of his bed. He opened the blanket box beneath the window, took from it a large polythene bag. The bag was beginning to smell, but not badly. He took a bone from the bag, placed it in front of Sparky; Sparky didn't move. He'd been trained over and over again. He wouldn't eat until his master said he could. Richard looked at the dog. "More trouble to me than your worth," he said. The dog cocked its head, looked up at him, saliva making a dewdrop on its lip. "Okay," Richard said quietly, "eat your bone." The dog relaxed forward, put its paws in front of its face, holding the bone at each end, and tucked in. Richard went to the door of his room and listened. Sometimes Deirdre would cry in the night from bad dreams, and sometimes their father was woken by her cries. But not tonight. The house was silent, the crunching of bones in the dog's teeth the only sound. Richard went back to the window, watched again.

"Don't you ever go off duty?" Ingeborg said. They were by the bridge again, Aveyard leaning over the parapet. "I followed you all the way down the Hill; you were like a man sleep-walking."

"I was thinking," he said, "anyway, what are you doing out at this time of night?"

"I couldn't sleep," she said, "I kept seeing that body, half in, half out of the water."

"And came down here to exorcise the memory of it?"

"No, I followed you."

She stood in front of him. He put his arms round her waist, drew her towards him. They didn't speak, didn't kiss or embrace, just clasped each other.

"First dead man you've ever seen?" he asked, gently.

"I saw my mother, but I was too young to remember what she looked like. Somehow, seeing Humphrey Holdeness down there, slumped over, half in the water . . . ! I've seen him many many times; I didn't much care for him, he wasn't the kind of man I could ever make a friend of, or even like; but somehow, seeing him there, so . . . defenceless . . ."

He resisted the temptation to draw her to him, to enfold her completely in his arms, to comfort her with banal words. "First dead man I saw," he said, "I couldn't sleep for three nights afterwards. Suddenly it all comes real, all the business about death, and the finality of it, all the knowledge that, whatever you do, you can't undo that one thing; they're gone, and that's it."

"And you, you have to find out why, and when, and who?"

"No, not why. When and who, where and with what, but never why. Police officers who look for the reasons tend to set themselves up as judges of men, and that clouds their vision. They can't be good policeman if they're continually making judgments of people."

"You wouldn't condemn a man like Holdeness? He hadn't much to recommend him, from what I've heard."

"He was alive, and now he's dead. The way he lived doesn't matter to me; I'm only interested in the way he died."

"What about you, and the way you live? Chasing dead men, spending your time with criminals? Aren't you afraid that's going to affect you? You say you don't judge people, but in the long run, isn't it bound to affect you? Won't you finish up despising people?"

Many people had said what she had just said to him. "I once investigated a very strange murder in a village not far from here," he said, "and do you know, I can only remember three people connected with that job. One's an old man called Wally—and for all I know Wally could be dead now and the other two, can you guess?"

"Sam Gainer and Cluney?"

"That's right. That's where I met them, and I've known

them ever since, and now I reckon Sam Gainer is one of my real friends. And Cluney, too, of course. You see, the human mind suppresses things it doesn't want; memory is selective. I forget all the bad things, all the bad people, and remember the good ones, the sincere genuine ones . . ."

"Will you remember me . . . ?"

Now he hugged her. "It's time you were in bed," he said. She looked hard at him. "Are we going to be friends?" she asked. "I hope so," he said.

"There's a lot to learn about each other, and you have the advantage of me, because you know what to ask and I don't. You're not married are you? Where do you live? Do you have a girl-friend? Does a policeman come home sharp at six, except when he's on a case . . ."

"Stop it," he said, placing a finger across her mouth. "We shall find out about each other, slowly. If we want to. Don't try to get too far, too quickly."

"I have a terrible feeling," she said, "there's not too much time. That's really why I couldn't sleep. It seemed such a waste . . ."

He drew her to him, kissed her hard on her mouth. Her lips moved beneath his; she tightened her arms around him, kissed him with an intensity equal to his own. They walked home together up Bent Hill and along Church Row. He watched her go into her father's cottage, waved to her when she turned at the door to wave to him. It was two o'clock.

CHAPTER ELEVEN

Sunday morning early. Jim Bruton turned up at the police station at seven, woke the inspector with a cup of Mrs Verney's tea. Aveyard sat up on the cot, rubbing sleep from his eyes. Dammit, he thought, how does Jim manage it. Jim Bruton looked as if he'd had twelve hours sound sleep. "When shall we get the autopsy report?" he asked. Any other man would have looked smug. Not Jim Bruton. "I collected it on my way in," he said.

"What does it say, in brief?"

"Broken neck, no other signs of violence."

"Any 'consistencies'?"

"Consistent with a fall from that bridge."

"No scalp wounds?"

"No, but soil impregnated in his hair."

It happens. A man falls, it doesn't have to be from a great height. The way he lands piles all his weight on the wrong place, dislocates one of the cervical vertebrae in what laymen call the neck. It happens to jumpers sometimes when they land in sand, men who fall off walls, buildings. Aveyard could see the picture; Holdeness standing with his back to the wall is pushed or falls over. The wall was only about twenty-four inches high. His knees would bend of course, his body would tend to arch forward. His hands would grab at the parapet, miss. His heels would scrape over the parapet, and he'd fall, flat on the top of his head. Because his body was arched slightly forward, his weight would snap two of the vertebrae apart. And that's it.

"So it was a push, or he fell. He couldn't have been drunk, not on four pints and a packet of crisps, and he didn't keep booze in the house." Aveyard struggled out of bed, stiff with the night's discomfort. "I'll bet they all plead guilty after a night in here," he said, "to get into a comfortable prison bed."

Mrs Verney'd grilled him a piece of bacon, and had made toast. "You'll have to forgive us," she said, "but we'd let the housekeeping go since we thought we'd be away on holiday." Thank God for a village shop that has a back door and is open day and night.

Sunday morning in a village is slow and smoke rises vertically from the chimneys in the absence of wind. The trees help. Most of the ovens are fired by coal since there's no gas in the village, old-fashioned three-ring stoves that stay hot day and night and heat the water, stoves warm enough to bathe in front of. Sunday mornings are bath mornings; Mam stokes the stove for the Sunday dinner and the menfolk have a damned good wash in a tin tub.

The Reverend Philip Morris conducts a service Sunday morning; not that you'd notice it. Veronica Scotia they call Ronnie is always there, sharp as a button, at eight o'clock. "A lot to do today," she tells the Lord during meditation, while the reverend is trying to recall the order of the service.

There's a cat mewing by the font, and illogically Ronnie thinks, "Poor thing, it wants to go out and do its business," but she sits there, and kneels when required by the order of things, and offers up her sinful soul to a merciful God. Philip Morris is aware that he hasn't cleaned his teeth; a raw onion for supper last night said to be good for stopping blood clots of which he's always afraid, but hell on the teeth in the morning. He really must talk to Marina today, really must get her to disclose the name of the Father, no, father with a small 'f', isn't it? The name of the Father with a capital F is well known to us all.

"That bloody dog," Robin Gotch shouted. Richard came running out of the back door, down the path to his father's workshop. He'd sneaked downstairs at six o'clock and let the dog out for a bit of a run and a cock-your-leg. Now his Dad'd go mad, chase the spaniel yapping all over the back garden until he caught it, and then rub its nose in it and throw the dog as far as he could. The dog always landed right. "This is the last time," Robin Gotch said, "the last time. You can't say I haven't warned you, I've told you about that dog until I'm blue in the face." Deirdre Gotch came to the back door. "Breakfast's ready when you two have stopped messing about!" she called. "I wonder if it's the bones making the dog go like that," Richard thought. "If you'd only show it a bit of affection," he said; "dogs need affection more than humans."

Robin Gotch was sorry, but couldn't bring himself to apologise to his son, his own son. "Clean it up after your breakfast then," he said. Richard put his hand on his Dad's arm. "I'm sorry," he said, "honest!" His Dad looked at his hand. "You cut yourself?" he asked, looking at the elastoplast bandage on his son's thumb. "Cutting bread, nothing serious, though it bled a lot." They went together into the house, into the Sunday morning smell of bacon, and fried bread.

Sunday morning Mrs Gibbins came out of the side door of the Hall, walked into the rose garden, cut a King's Ransom, yellow in full bloom. Carefully, one by one, she prised the thorns off the stem which was about ten inches long. She was wearing a black skirt, a black blouse spattered with paint. On her head was the only hat she could find, a man's straw trilby. She walked down the rise of the Hall garden, past the baobab, past the ailanthus, heading towards the lake, carrying the rose in her hand. The Hall was surrounded by a high wall, broken only where Bent Hill crossed the stream. When she got level with the bridge she took a sighting from the baobab back to the top corner of the grounds, where the crown and sceptre ornament still stood on the wall. She turned to the right, sighted from the ailanthus to a room at the far corner of the Hall itself, walked, as if on a bearing until both sitings coincided. She stood still at the point where the lines would have crossed, had such lines been drawn. Then she turned again. There was a conifer high on West Lodge Hill, a small conifer by the drive that led up to the Hall. She moved a pace to her left, sighting one conifer exactly on the other. Then she bent down. She could see where the turf had been replaced. She pushed the rose into the ground, exactly at her feet, between the tips of her shoes. She had been a virgin when she came to the house in response to an advertisement for a housekeeper. The Comte de Vaspail, the most charming man she'd ever met, filled the house with Frenchmen, chefs from Maxims, sales men, engineers, noblemen, doctors, advocates—much better than the English word 'lawyers'. Oddly enough there were few 'artists'. Then Jacques Borel came, a second son of a nobleman, weak, disappointed at not being a first son, vain, unreliable, but oh, so devastatingly beautiful. It was the first time she had known a man could be beautiful. Their child was born after he had been dropped by parachute near Toulouse into a German ambush. "Our baby," the Frenchmen called it, and rallied round. The doctor helped her deliver it, all vied with each other to amuse and keep it happy. It lived for two years, then died. Only one person in the village proper knew about it, Nellie Binns, and she was as secretive as a stone. By the time the baby died, the French had left Bent Hall, one by one, even the Comte, and Nellie it was who helped her bury it here, where the pine touches the pine, the crown and sceptre touch the baobab, and the ailanthus points to the Hall, to the top corner bedroom, in which the child had been conceived and two years later had died.

Arthur Binns slowly wheezed up the last step of the flight of steps. "I ought to have brought her downstairs," he thought for the hundredth time. "I would have brought her downstairs, but she likes her bedroom." He pushed open the bedroom door, which squeaked. "I must get the oil can," he thought, also for the hundredth time. It was chilly in the bedroom for a June morning. The room faced north, didn't get the morning sun. He went across the room to the heavy green chenille curtains that effectively cut off the light, slowly dragged them aside on their brass rings. One of the pins that held the curtain to the rings had come unfastened. "I'll get a chair and get up to that today," he thought. He walked over to the bed. Double bed, a family bed. They'd made Samantha in that bed, he thought, then chided himself for the vulgarity. Dammit, he'd left on his reading glasses, couldn't focus properly. He must hunt out the other glasses case this morning, and then he could carry both pairs in his waistcoat pocket, one on, one in his pocket. As he walked nearer, the bed came into better focus, and he could see Nellie's head on the pillow, make out her features in the strong morning light. Her eyes were closed, her hands were laid down the counterpane, still, all skin and knuckle. He stood beside the bed. "I must change that pillow case for her today," he thought, "and give her a clean glass for her teeth." He raised his hand to brush a wisp of hair from her forehead. She opened her eyes, smiled at him, as best she could. "Is it morning?"

"Sunday. Joanna will be here soon."

"I haven't heard the bells?"

"It's early. Is there anything you want?"

"No, love. Joanna'll get my breakfast."

So she would; half a slice of bread dipped in warm milk, two spoonsful of tea. One green pill to help the breathing, another to stop the heart pains. "You ought to go to Church," she said, "it'd give you something to do."

"I've got to put a pin in that curtain."

"You could oil the door while you're at it?"

"Yes, I must do that. I'll just have my breakfast first, and then I'll get right on with it."

"Have your breakfast first," she said as she closed her eyes.

"It's good to have young Bill Aveyard round the place again," Sam said. Cluney clucked. "How can you say a thing like that," she said, "I mean, it's all right when he comes over for a meal, but not when he's working here. Anybody'd think you enjoy crime?" she said.

"Better than reading about it in the Sunday paper!"

"He seems to get on all right with Ingeborg."

He looked up at her. "Woman," he said, "a man no sooner puts his arm round a girl's waist than you're running him down the aisle."

"I waited long enough for you to start running!" she said. Marriage has its own language of affection, badinage the traced veil of man's emotions.

She sat on a stool beside his chair. "Can we have a talk," she said. Words of serious intent. "The Dutch always painted pregnant women sitting down," he said, "somehow a pregnant woman looks specially attractive when she sits down. The lines are better. Serious talk? That means about the baby?"

"Yes," she said. "I'm not really worried about it, you know, but we have to consider all the possibilities, and women of my age who have children do have things that go wrong."

"I know," he said, "I've thought about it."

"Could you have a word with Dr Samson. I mean, it's in his hands, isn't it, and if I'd never actually *seen* the baby . . ."

"Listen to me, my dear," he said. "Some things are better not talked about too much. Some things are better not spelled out. Anything we say to each other is going to be a fact we've got to live with for the rest of our lives together. Some questions are better not asked, some promises shouldn't be sought. You know how I feel about you, you know how much I want to safeguard you, and protect you. But don't ask me any questions, will you?"

She thought for a moment, then patted his knee. "You're right," she said.

The police car brought Baines and Peter Berris to the Bent police station. Peter Berris was nineteen, lived at number 4, Aisle Cottages, Welby. By occupation he was a shop assistant for a firm in Birton that sold men's clothing.

"Got all that down, Baines, have you?"

Baines nodded, fatigued, miserable.

"Now I'd be obliged, Mr Berris, if you'd tell me all about your trip to Birton on that bus, starting with the first memory you have of seeing the girl we think is Mrs Holdeness. Take your time, miss nothing out, every little detail may help us. And take it easy, because I'm sure Constable Baines here will want to take notes."

Sergeant Bruton grinned. Aveyard was a right bastard, but he'd given Baines a short sharp lesson he'd not forget in a hurry, made a better detective of him, overnight.

Berris's account was clear. He'd seen Mrs Holdeness waiting at the bus stop, he'd waved goodbye to her when the London coach pulled out of the Birton station. She'd been distressed, he'd helped her as much as he could. The *pram*, well it was more of a *push chair*, had been folded and put under the stairs. It had a carri-cot that could be lifted away from the chassis. In the carri-cot was a baby.

Aveyard interrupted him. Had he actually seen a baby, or was there a bundle of clothing and bedding he'd assumed was a baby? That's right, come to think of it, he hadn't actually seen a baby's face. See a bundle in a carri-cot where a baby should be and automatically you assume it's a baby. It would have needed another mother, sitting on the bench beside the cot, to say "what a pity to have him covered up on a day like this, let him breathe, poor little mite." But Peter Berris had none of that special reality at nineteen.

"Where was the carri-cot while you were giving Mrs Holdeness tea at the buffet?"

"On the London coach, keeping her seat for her."

"And the bundle?"

"In the carri-cot!"

Mothers don't leave their children like that, their own flesh and blood. Not babies born deformed, especially! Not any children they care about, and the evidence was that, whatever her marriage to Humphrey may have been, Samantha really did care for Christine.

After Peter Berris and Baines had left, the sergeant read through the notes he had taken independently. Evidence is like plum pudding, heavy, stodgy. But there is the occasional currant.

"Two things, apart from the baby . . ." Aveyard said.

"Fran is lying when he says he saw Mrs Holdeness on to the bus . . ."

"If you look at the notes I gave you," Aveyard said, "I think what he said was 'I waited with her until I could see the bus coming. I watched her get on the bus. I waited until the bus was out of sight'. He didn't say where he was, did he? He waited until he saw the bus coming, then he drew back. Peter Berris hasn't said a word about seeing anyone else at the bus stop. Where was Fran? Why didn't he wait 'at' the bus stop, that's the natural thing to do, isn't it?"

"I would have thought so," Jim Bruton said. "Unless you didn't want to be seen?"

"Unless you were carrying something, a bundle, you didn't want to be seen!"

Bruton shook his head. "That's pure speculation, Inspector," he said.

"Well, do *you* believe the baby was in the carri-cot?"

"I don't know. I shan't know until we can find somebody who's actually seen that baby's face. We'll go for the conductor of that London coach, of course. The baby couldn't go all the way to London without having its face uncovered. If we discover she didn't touch the 'bundle' while she was on that coach, we shall have a good indication there was no baby in it . . ."

"There's another possibility, Jim, have you thought of that?"

"Yes, I have, but I didn't want to be the one to put it into words. The baby could have been dead. She could have been carrying a dead baby with her!"

Both were silent for a moment, horrified by the morbid thought. Finally, "There is one other thing," the sergeant said, "and this may have a bearing on everything else!" He read from his notes.

Inspector: She opened her bag and got out a twenty packet of cigarettes, you say. Did you have a chance to see anything else in the bag? Letters, a wallet, another twenty packet?

Berris: Now you come to mention it, Inspector, of course I didn't think anything of it at the time because anybody travelling, well they'd go to the bank and get a bit extra, wouldn't they, but when she put the cigarette packet back in her bag I saw she had a whole wad of notes in there, you know, the new ten-pound notes. We don't see too many of them and I . . .

Inspector: Could you make a guess how many there were?

Berris: There must have been,let me think, oh yes, there'd be all of forty. She must have had the thick end of four hundred quid in that handbag . . .

Sunday morning Cheryl and Amanda Minsell spend with the horses. Not surprising; every spare moment the two girls spend with their horses. They got up at seven o'clock; Heidi and Gladys were fractious after the warm night and didn't want to be caught. Amanda fetched a half bucket of oats from the feed shed, rattled its side. Both horses cantered up to her, both trying to put their noses in the bucket at the same time. It was the work of a second for Cheryl to slip a head collar on each, but by then the bucket was emptied of oats. An hour's grooming, twenty minutes tail pulling—Cheryl was plaiting a ring for her hair and the horses were providing the raw materials, very much against their will—and the horses could be saddled.

"Look at your tack, Amanda," Cheryl said, "it's filthy." The whole difference between the two girls was summed up by the way they kept horse tack; Amanda was quick, light, deft, not very thorough, Cheryl slower, heavier, and had a preoccupation with detail. Both mounted, walked their horses round the paddock, warming them up. Then Amanda, impatient, kicked Gladys into a trot, then a canter in figures of eight.

"On the wrong leg," Cheryl called. She squeezed with her knees, gave Heidi the merest flick with her heel, and Heidi followed Gladys, cantering on the right leg perfectly. A low gate separated the paddock from the far yard. Twice round the paddock, trot and canter, canter and trot, and then Cheryl headed Heidi towards the gate, leaped neatly over. Amanda followed, on Gladys. "Come on, you old bitch," she muttered, her teeth clenched. Gladys approached the gate at a fast canter. "Slow her down," Cheryl called, but Amanda couldn't hear. At the last second, however, Gladys made her own decision, stopped her canter, dug her front legs into the ground and slid to a stop, her chest almost touching the top rail of the gate.

"Hang on, Amanda," Cheryl shouted, but it was too late. Amanda had nothing to hang on to and slid forward along the horse's neck, tumbling over its head in a welter of arms and legs. Cheryl dismounted rapidly, tied Heidi's rein to a hay rake, and rushed over to where her sister lay groaning, entangled in the bars of the gate on to which she'd fallen. Gladys stood contentedly, head down, nibbling grass. Cheryl raised her crop, gave it a belt over the nose. "You silly bastard," she said. The horse reared, galloped away, its reins dangling. Cheryl pulled her sister away from the gate. "You all right?" she asked, anxious. Amanda groaned, tried to stand up, "I think I've twisted my ankle," she said. Cheryl helped her across the farmyard, sat her on hay bales, dragged off her jodhpur boot, and tried to pull her jodhpurs up her leg. The ankle ached, but when Cheryl wriggled it, there was no sign of extra pain.

"Nothing's broken," she said, "just a sprain. Can you grab hold of my shoulder, and I'll get you in and put a cold bandage on it for you."

She assisted her sister into the house; Doug Minsell looked at the ankle, confirmed Cheryl's diagnosis. Mrs Minsell prepared a cold compress, gave Amanda two aspirins, and packed her off to bed grumbling.

Cheryl helped her sister take off her riding clothes, get into bed. "What a bother," Amanda said, "and all over a little sprain. I wanted to go up to the police station this morning, tell that groovy inspector what we talked about, what I saw by the bridge."

"I don't suppose it matters, anyway," Cheryl said. "You stay in bed today, and we can go up there and tell him tomorrow. Anyway, if you like, I could go up and tell him for you . . ."

"Don't you dare!" Amanda said. "I saw it, not you! It's my story, not yours. Don't you dare!"

"No use putting it off," Aveyard said. "Shall we have her in?"

"If we go down there, we'll have four kids and her husband to contend with."

"She'll be cooking breakfast for them, I suppose?"

"She's got a daughter old enough to cope. I'll go and fetch her," Jim Bruton said.

Aveyard was sitting on his own when the telephone rang. He answered it. "Bent police station."

"Inspector Aveyard, and quick about it, lad."

"This is Inspector Aveyard, and less of your lad!"

It was the pathologist. "Lesson number one, don't make assumptions," he said with a chuckle, "and that's the second one I've made in twenty-four hours. My apologies, Inspector!" Sunday morning chit chat, what the hell?

"What's the second assumption, sir?" Aveyard asked.

"You remember we identified the human blood on that sawdust sample?"

"Yes, sir, I was there, remember?"

"So you were. Tell me, did you assume, as I did, the bone also was human?"

"Yes, sir, of course I did!"

"Well, so did I, and we were both mistaken. The blood was human, the bone came from a horse. It suddenly occurred to me during dinner last night that we tested for human blood and when that turned out positive we left it. I couldn't sleep last night thinking about it, and this morning I ran another series, for other animal sources. I got a positive for horse!"

"You're certain?"

"That rabbit serum never fails. It's we humans who leave the gaps."

Aveyard hung up, his mind buzzing. Human blood, horse's bones. It didn't make sense, it didn't bloody well make sense. Falstaff finds bones in the grounds of the Hall that turn out to be human, from a child two years old, buried in war-time; they find a woman and her two-year-old child are missing, but are reported to have left the village on a bus, which report they haven't yet been able to confirm; they find the husband has been having it off with a married woman in the village and that appears to be common knowledge even to the husband himself; sawdust under a bench has human blood and horse's bones in it, and the saw couldn't be used by any but the three people who work there, and none of them has a cut anywhere, that was the first thing they had checked. The husband of the missing woman dies of a broken neck, after he and the married woman have virtually disappeared for a half an hour, in a village literally teeming with folks. What kind of a bloody case is this, he thought, angrily. The phone rang again. "I thought if I were to speak to you myself, it might prevent you dragging me out of the garden later," the Chief said.

"I was just going to phone you."

"I had a feeling you were. What progress are you making?"

"Absolutely none."

The Chief chuckled silently. "I've just had a word with the pathologist," he said. "I'll bet that has you baffled?"

"It has, Chief!"

"Have they got a butcher in Bent?"

"Yes, Chief." Aveyard fumbled with the sergeant's papers. "Wilkins, shop next door to Sam Gainer."

"Your old friend, eh? I should talk with Sam if I were you. And look inside that butcher's shop." He hung up. Aveyard could hear the click cut off the Chief's chuckle.

The sergeant came in, with Mrs Cevicec. Aveyard rose, showed her to a seat. The sergeant sat at the table at the back, a notebook open before him. When Aveyard had seen she was comfortable, he sat down. He put his hands together, looking at them. Then he looked at Mrs Cevicec. There was a half smile on her face, but whether of superiority or apprehension it would be hard to say.

"As you know," Aveyard began, "Mr Holdeness was found dead last evening." Her expression didn't alter. Dammit, don't say she was going to be a tough one. "I have reason to believe," Aveyard continued, "that you and Mr Holdeness were on intimate terms, and that you were somewhere near the place where Mr Holdeness's body was found?"

"I was there," she said, "I walked over that actual bridge." Aveyard lifted his hand, old for his years. "Don't say anything at all," he said, "until I've finished. Believe me, it'll be in your best interests to hear what I have to say before you speak."

She pursed her lips, but the smile didn't change.

"We have reason to believe you were in the vicinity about the time he died. I am conducting an investigation into the matter of Mr Holdeness's death, and as part of that investigation, it is my duty to question you. I have no reason at this moment to suspect that you have committed any offence, and at this moment it is not my intention to arrest you. I have merely asked you to come here to the police station to make matters easier for both of us. My sergeant will listen to what you have to say and make notes for our guidance. Do you understand that?"

"Everything will be taken down and used in evidence against me, is that what you're saying?" she asked.

"No, that's specifically what I am *not* saying. I am merely asking questions at the moment, and the sergeant is making notes to remind us of your answers. If, during the course of those questions, I have reason to suspect you of any crime, I shall stop asking questions, and caution you in the appropriate manner. The sergeant will take a written record of anything you may care to say, though you won't be obliged to say anything."

"But at the moment, I'm just helping you with your enquiries?"

"That's right."

"We'll begin, then?" she said, brazen.

"I'm ready, Mrs Cevicec, I just wanted to make quite certain you knew what we are doing! Now, did you see Mr Holdeness last evening?"

"Yes."

"Where?"

"Bent Hill."

"You met by previous arrangement."

"That's right."

"Do you know what time it was when you met?"
"Ten o'clock."
"May I ask you how you know what time it was? Do you wear a watch?"
She looks surprised, he thought, now why should that be?
"The church clock," she said, "it was striking ten."
Dammit. Aveyard had heard that church clock strike every hour since he came into the village, and this was the first time he'd ever been conscious of the fact there was a church clock that struck. How easy to overlook the simple things.
"Of course," he said, "I just wanted to make certain you'd noticed it . . ." Why hadn't he noticed it, standing on the bridge with Ingeborg? Dammit, the clock not only struck the hours, it pounded out every quarter.
"So you met at ten o'clock. What did you do then?"
"We went for a bit of a walk."
"Where?"
"In the grounds of the Hall."
"Down the path by the bridge?"
"That's right."
"And what did you do after your walk?"
"We came back to the bridge. Don't you want to know where we'd been, what we'd been doing?" she asked.
Temper, watch it. "No, I don't, Mrs Cevicec," he said, emphasising her married name. Oh, Bill Aveyard, you prude. You don't want her to tell you about it, do you? Second-hand sex knowledge, dirty post-card stuff. You've looked at plenty in your time! "I am merely concerned with your whereabouts. I may need to be concerned with your activities later, but I sincerely hope not." Watch it, you're doing better with this witness than you've any right, so don't mess it up by being snide. She's what she is, no need to put a name to it, no need for subjective

judgments. You wouldn't touch her with Binns' barge-pole, but don't let her realise that, or she'll clam up, and then where will you be?

"You came back to the bridge. Mr Holdeness and you. Did you go away together, or did you separate?"

"I went home. I had to get my husband's supper."

"Mr Holdeness stayed there?"

"I really couldn't say!"

Watch it. One wrong word and you've lost your witness.

"When you left him at the bridge, where was he? Actually on the bridge, or on the road leading to the bridge?"

"He was, like, on it."

"Just standing there?"

"Yes."

"You said 'right, I'll be getting home' or something like that, and turned round and walked away."

"Something like that."

What did you actually say, you sexy bitch, "keep your flies buttoned up," something like *that*? Aveyard didn't want to know.

"And you didn't turn back, to look at him, wave good-night?"

"No, I was in a hurry to get home."

"What time did you get home?"

"I've forgotten," she said, "but your sergeant took a note of it when I could remember so he'd know, wouldn't he?" Wide-eyed innocence. She didn't want to be trapped.

"Shall I look it up?" Jim Bruton asked.

"I don't think that'll be necessary."

"I'm sorry I can't remember," she said. She's rubbing it in, the bitch. Forget it, don't lose your temper.

"Mrs Cevicec, I want you to think very carefully and tell me exactly what Mr Holdeness's condition was like when you left him?"

"He was tired, I can promise you that."

"What was his *mental* condition? Did he show any signs of depression. Did he say anything about his wife having left him?"

"She couldn't give him the time of day!"

"Was he depressed?"

"Not particularly. We'd had it, so he was a bit tired!"

"Did you have any reason, any reason at all, thinking back about it, to suspect he might take his own life?"

"Him? Kill 'isself? He wasn't brave enough for that, I can tell you. All talk, that's what he was, take my word for it."

Aveyard looked at Jim Bruton, but there was no help there. Bruton was obviously as baffled as Aveyard was.

"Well, I think that's all," Aveyard said, "unless there's anything else you want to tell me?"

She rose to go. She was still wearing a pinafore, clutching a purse in her hand. She smoothed the front of the pinafore.

"Is he going to give me a ride back?" she said. "I've got a lot to do this morning." Aveyard beckoned to the sergeant. "Send the car," he said, "and you come back here." She didn't need an escort. She opened the door for herself. "There's one thing you haven't asked me," she said as she prepared to go out.

"Oh yes," Aveyard said, "and what's that?"

"Who was the man I saw walking towards the bridge down Bent Hill as I turned to leave Humphrey and go home. When he saw me looking, he ducked into the hedge, but I know who he was, all right! I'd reckonise that pansy walk anywhere!"

"I wasn't there," Malcolm Minton said, "what's she trying to do to me, the bitch. I wasn't there, I wasn't there, and I won't say any more until I've seen my lawyer. You have no right . . ."

"Where were you?"

"I was at home, ask Fran. I *was* at home, wasn't I, Fran, wasn't I?" And Fran nodded. "All evening," he confirmed.

"We played bezique all evening, didn't we, Fran. I've kept the scores, I can show them to you."

"Come on, sergeant," Aveyard said, "let's get out of here."

As they walked out of the house called Tolly's, the church bells stopped ringing. A thousand birds in the trees below the house took their place, and sang. Now the morning was warm; half past ten. "Fancy a cup of coffee?" Aveyard asked the sergeant. No need for a reply. They'd left the car by the Rectory gate at the end of the lane. "Down to the shop," Aveyard told the driver, as he and the sergeant climbed into the back.

Cluney gave them coffee. Blue Mountain, from Jamaica. "You live well in the villages?" Aveyard quipped. "Oddly enough," Sam said, "we get it wholesale from an Algerian in Derby!"

"Supper last night, fit for a gourmet?"

"Bits and pieces, and the mystery ingredient!"

"What's that?"

"Cluney's cooking." She was passing on her way to sit down, and he slapped her rump. "I've put on a stone since I married her!" "So have I," she said, laughing.

"You ought to eat more meat!" Aveyard said, "that'd keep your weight down. Good steaks, lamb cutlets. You with a butcher right next door, a fellow tradesman, you get it at wholesale price,I suppose."

Sam looked at Cluney, looked back at Aveyard. "I know

you too well for you to try that on with me," he said. "If you want to ask me questions about our neighbour, ask 'em straight out, and don't shilly-shally around."

"I don't know what you're talking about," Aveyard protested, innocence outraged! Or so he pretended. The sergeant smiled at him, put down his cup. "I think Mr Gainer's got you there, Inspector."

"And you could go back to being a constable, you know!" It was a meaningless threat, a token of their rapport. "What kind of a butcher is he?" Aveyard asked.

"I don't buy any meat from him, if that tells you anything. The day he starts having deliveries in broad daylight, I might start going in there."

"When's the last time you saw him?"

"He was in today. We open for an hour of a Sunday morning. It's funny what people forget. Mostly cigarettes and sweets, but we sell the occasional tin of creamed rice, half a pound of cheese, a bottle of HP sauce for the Sunday dinner. They'd need it, on his meat!"

"Think hard, Sam. By any chance had Mr Wilkins cut his finger?"

"Cut his finger? What on earth has that to do . . ."

"Don't try to work it out; just try to visualise him again. Had he cut his finger? Was he wearing a bandage?"

Sam thought, hard. "No," he said finally. "No, he hadn't. Well, let me put it this way since you're such a stickler for accuracy—or rather your sergeant is. He wasn't wearing a bandage on either hand, and I was able to see both his hands up to the wrist. I can remember, distinctly, he put his hands on the top of the showcase, both of 'em. And neither one had a bandage on it."

"Not even one of these flesh-coloured elastoplasts?"

"Well, they call 'em flesh-coloured, but you can see 'em. Young Richard Gotch, he bought a packet the other day, and you put it on for him, didn't you, Cluney?"

"Yes, you can see them," she said, "though they're better than the old-fashioned dark-coloured ones."

"Cuts on fingers, butchers who have night-time deliveries, what the devil are you after, you young fox?" Sam Gainer asked.

Aveyard rose, the sergeant, on cue, rose with him. "Thank you for the coffee," he said. The sergeant murmured 'thank you' and they went out together, through the shop, into the forecourt which overlooked the green.

Anne and Rupert Sudbury were riding past, on a tandem. Cheryl rode down New Farm Road on her horse. When Cheryl saw the policeman, she waved, almost stopped, then changed her mind, kicked her horse up into a trot, rising and falling in the saddle with infinite grace. The bungalow front gardens, across the Green, were buzzing with the whirr of petrol-driven grass cutters. Virginia Nasset was cutting roses. A man Aveyard had not met was carting wheelbarrows of manure from a pile Doug Minsell had dumped earlier on the road outside his bungalow. Laszlo Cevicec who earned a spare bob or two with his spade, was digging the border at the side of the lawn on the second bungalow from the top, almost opposite the corner of the Green. Aveyard and the sergeant turned right, walked slowly over the Bent Road past the pub. 'Horse bones and human blood," the sergeant said, "and young Richard Gotch keeps a dog and wears an elastoplast on his finger."

"Horse bones'd be big," Aveyard said, "and young Gotch's dad's a carpenter. You see the mistake we've all made, don't you?"

"Now that you've come to mention it . . ."

"Don't worry, it's easy to be wise after the event."

Because sawdust beneath a saw had been found to contain bone dust and blood, everyone had assumed the bone dust had been created by that saw.

"Like to have a word with your son, if you don't mind, Mr Gotch."

"What's the young bugger been up to?" his father said.

Richard was in the back garden, sitting in a deck chair, reading the Sunday newspaper, the dog at his feet. As Aveyard and the sergeant came through the house, the dog ran towards them, yapping. "Shut that bloody noise, you daft bugger," Gotch said. His dislike of the animal was obvious. When the dog persisted, he aimed a kick at it which fortunately the dog escaped. Richard dashed across the lawn with a lead and choker chain which he slipped round the dog's neck. He quietened the dog, which obeyed his command instantly, took it and secured it to the fence. Sergeant Bruton noticed the dog trembled as he led it past his father.

"I must have been mad," Gotch said, "to let him have that thing. I only agreed when I'd had a drop too much, and it was here the next day."

Richard came and stood in front of them, a schoolboy on the carpet. "Cut your finger," Aveyard said without preamble, "how did that happen, lad?"

"Cutting bread. The knife slipped."

"You ought to be more careful," his dad said, "and learn to handle tools."

"When was that?" Aveyard persisted.

"Friday. Tea time."

"I thought our Deirdre made the tea Friday?"

"I helped her cut the bread."

"Can you tell me what you were doing Friday?" Aveyard asked.

"I can tell you," his Dad said, "for once he was helping me. I got home from work at ten past five as I allus do, and he came with me up the wood-yard to get some oak they'd promised me. And a right price that Cattell charges for it."

"And it was before that you were making tea?"

"No, he weren't," his father interrupted, "he was sky-larking about down at the shop. I sent our Deirdre to look for him. When she came back with him we went up to the wood-yard and she set about making the tea."

"Is that your workshop?" Aveyard asked, indicating the prefabricated building erected in the garden.

"That's right. My hobby, you might say, carpentry." His pride was obvious.

"Is it really? The sergeant here's a dab hand at carpentry, aren't you, sergeant?" Bruton nodded, amazed, He wouldn't know one end of a chisel from the other. "I bet he'd like to see your workshop, wouldn't you, sergeant?" Bruton nodded again. "Oh, yes," he said, "nothing would interest me more, if you've got the time, Mr Gotch." Mr Gotch was half way to the workshop, key in hand.

Aveyard watched them walk inside.

"I see your Dad keeps his key in his pocket," Aveyard said, "where do you keep yours?"

"I don't know what you mean."

"Yes, you do, lad, you've got a key to that place."

"How do you know?"

"Just say a little rabbit told me."

Richard was scuffing the ground with the toe of his shoe.

"You won't tell him?" he said.

"Why do you think I got rid of him. My sergeant couldn't care less about carpentry." Richard Gotch smiled. "Really?" he asked.

"It's all because of the dog, isn't it?" Richard nodded. "Let's see if I've got it right. You have this dog your dad doesn't like. You go down to the back of the butcher's shop at night, and you steal bones. Well, it's not really stealing, and I don't intend to prosecute you for that. You brought these bones home, but they're too big for such a little dog, so you take 'em in your father's workshop there, and cut 'em up on his saw. Right so far?"

"Right," Richard said.

"And presumably, being a tidy boy, you clean up the bone dust after you've used his saw . . ."

"It's a different colour. If he found that, he'd go mad, me using his workshop and his saw. Especially for something for the dog. I've asked him to make a kennel, but he won't."

"Now, getting back to last Friday. You'd cut the bones, or you were cutting them, and you caught your thumb on the power saw, right?"

"Nicked the end. Oh, not much, but crikey, it didn't half bleed!"

"I'll bet it did. Anyway, you knew your Dad would soon be home, so you had to sweep up the bone dust, and you stuck your finger in the sawdust to stop it bleeding, right?"

"Yes, it was the only way. I had a bit of a polythene bag I always put the sweepings in; I put all the stuff in there, kept my thumb in it until I could get down to the shop. I knew they sold elastoplast, and Mrs Gainer would look after me."

"She stuck an elastoplast on it for you?"

"Yes. Sam Gainer sprinkled pepper on it; that stopped the bleeding."

"And then your sister Deirdre turned up, and said your Dad wanted you. No time to dispose of the plastic bag. You came home, went with your Dad to the wood-yard to collect the oak with the bag in your pocket, saw your chance, and emptied it in the sawdust under the saw; is that it?"

"You're a genius," Richard said, "how on earth did you work all that out? That's it, exactly right."

"I've been a policeman for a week or two," Aveyard

said, ruffling his feathers. "You won't tell Dad," Richard pleaded, "he'd make me get rid of the dog." There was the whine of the power saw from inside the shed.

"Take my advice," Aveyard said, "buy your bones from another butcher, and make sure he gives you small ones you don't need to cut up on your dad's saw, because, if your dad ever catches you at it, there'll be hell to pay." The workshop door opened. Gotch and the sergeant came out. The sergeant nodded at Aveyard. "Bright lad your sergeant," Gotch said, "he's just shown me how to grease the saw blade using a candle. According to your sergeant, it makes the blade cut a treat. In all my years, I've never heard about that." "Ah, a little candle wax can hide a whole skeleton of bones . . ." the sergeant said, winking at Richard.

"Want to come to Chaldwell this afternoon," Flemming asked her, "in the cab with me and my dad?"

"You'll be lucky! If it was a Lotus . . ."

"I'll have a Lotus one of these days. The business comes to me, you know. Lots of money in timber!"

"Who cares about money?"

"You can't get a Lotus without it."

"Anyway, I've got a date this afternoon."

"Who with?"

"None of your business; but we shan't be looking at stands of timber, and he won't have his dad with him," Marina said.

CHAPTER TWELVE

Dinner time Sunday in the village, but police work still. Back in Birton the pathologists, forensic scientists on overtime, check the Holdeness autopsy, blood bone sawdust, the old bones Falstaff found. Infra red, ultra violet; microtones and microtone sections, everything under the probing eye of microscopes. After the horse bone and human blood oversight, nothing is left to chance, nothing omitted. On Sunday the canteen's closed but they make do with sandwiches and instant coffee made in a beaker. "Mind you wash it carefully, that's had blood in it!" They're all casual in this department of death; it doesn't do to be delicate when your next job may be dust under dead fingernails. Quiet constables from the detective department check at the bus station, the railway, long-distance coaches. Men like chameleons mingle with any crowd, masters of the art of asking questions without seeming to. "Busy tonight!" "What are you talking about, yesterday there was only one on!" "Women shouldn't travel alone!" "I kept my eye on her, I could see she'd been crying!" "Nice colour, that blue!" "This one wore green!" In the buffet, flash a photograph taken ten years ago and hope to God somebody, just once, will remember a face in the crowd. "Looks like our Nellie," but it isn't, couldn't possibly be. They're lucky, an Indian restaurant on Sheep Street defiles the Sabbath by serving curry. Now that Holdeness is dead, finding his wife and daughter become imperative, ears, eyes, nose, colour of hair, height, age, special characteristics; just a few variables but multiply each by the other and you've as much chance as winning the pools.

In the village the local press had been and gone; accidental death their quick grateful decision. Who likes to work on a Sunday when there's no need, and there's no news in death unless its murder, or there's violence, or you've served on a committee. MAN FOUND DEAD IN VILLAGE STREAM, the headline would read, then FOUL PLAY NOT SUSPECTED. If the overnight man got any more news he could knock out the word 'suspected', and substitute 'not ruled out'. The same number of letters in 'ruled out' but mustn't give them problems. Dear dead departed, even your mother didn't love you, poor bastard. SHOCK FIND FOR OFF-DUTY POLICEMAN. Give 'em a touch of the old human angle.

At *eleven o'clock on Saturday evening, Detective Inspector Bill Aveyard (33) of Birton police visiting Bent on a social visit,* no that's no good, two *visits* in one sentence, strike *'visiting'* insert *'in'* . . . *in Bent on a social visit, discovered,* no *saw, the body of Humphrey Holdeness (32) of 15 West Lodge Road, Bent, lying dead in a stream beneath a bridge on Bent Hill.* No, strike the *'dead'*, he didn't discover him or see him lying dead. He saw him lying. *Later he ascertained the body was dead,* but they won't like *'ascertained'*, will they? . . . *lying in a stream beneath a bridge on Bent Hill. On investigation the body proved to be dead.* That's good, it'll give the subs something to cut. *Police are searching for Mrs Holdeness who left home with her daughter on Wednesday last.* Can't leave it like that; it suggests she's done a bunk, and though we all know she's done a bunk we mustn't leave ourselves open to a libel action, must we? Got it, add *for an unknown destination.* That means she's gone somewhere but we don't know where, and doesn't necessarily imply she's done a bunk, though anybody with his head screwed on will know! *Foul play is not suspected,* and wrap it up with, *A public inquest will be held in the near future.* Nobody's said so, but they're bound to have an inquest, aren't they? Right, 'phone it in, then off to the pub for a game of crib.

Sunday dinners are cooking all over Bent, but when the village hears about Wilkins and his meat source, a lot of cold 'beef' set by for a wash-day Monday will not be eaten. The Reverend Philip Morris has finished his morning stint of Service; he's sitting in the library of the beautiful Old Rectory with his feet in a bowl of hot water. Sunday mornings, he always reserves for cutting his toe-nails, and hot water makes them pliable. The Women's Institute used to meet in this room; it's forty feet long and over twenty wide; there are bookshelves floor to ceiling on one side, and the other three walls are decorated in russet, gold, and white in the classical tradition. The high ceiling's painted white with blue panels and a frieze of gold intertwined leaves. It was far too good a room for the Women's Institute, he ruled, when first he came into the Living. The Living's dead now, and they'll never know who or what killed it! The numbers of the congregation could often be counted on the fingers of one hand, not including the thumb. Or one foot, he thought, snipping away at the in-growing nail of his big toe, in the elegant classical library. Cyprus sherry on the butler's tray, and a set of Beardsley's 'penis' prints are hidden, with the Last Exit behind

Cobbett's 'Rides'. Marina came into the library, wandering aimlessly. Thank the Lord nothing was yet showing of her pregnancy.

"You're going to have to tell your mother and me who the father is," he said. "Something will *Have* to be *Done!*"

There was a stack of old parish magazines on an inlaid table, pictures of the Church traced on a stencil with a ball point pen that leaked, and run off on the Church's stencilling machine, that also leaked. They hadn't had a magazine since Philip Morris came. He rose to his feet and walked to where she was, his wet foot leaving the print of the entire length of his sole on the parquet floor.

"You're flat footed," she said, giggling, "you've got fallen arches."

He seized her by the shoulders, shook her to stop her laughter. "I don't seem to be able to make you understand the Seriousness of what you've done!" he said, his voice shrill. "I know," she said, "I'm a fornicator and a harlot!"

"Don't be so bloody silly," he said, "I'm not talking about that! We've got a Good Living here, we're Comfortable, we've got a Good Way of Life, but do you think they'll let me Stay if you start having Babies before you're Married? Do you? They'll have me out of here like a shot, and then where do you think we'll get to?" She looked at him, wide-eyed. "Where *will* we be?" "In some slum parish in Birton," he said.

"It'd be better than this dead-and-alive hole."

He shook her again. "You're not to say that," he shrieked, his voice shrill in anger, "this is *not* a dead-and-alive hole. How much do you think this house would cost us to buy, have you ever thought of that? We live in it free! It doesn't cost us a penny. Who do you think paid for you to go to private school? Me? I couldn't have afforded anything like that. These dead-and-alive people, my parishioners, they paid for your school, in one way and another. Have you no gratitude, girl?"

He let his hands fall from her shoulders, stood back, quite exhausted by his paroxysm of anger. She turned listlessly from him, thumbed the top copy of the parish magazine.

"All I want to know," he said, quietly, "is the name of the lad who got you into trouble. . . ."

She had started to laugh. "Oh, you're so old-fashioned," she said, "Got me into trouble . . . I'm not in trouble, as you put it. I'm pregnant. Any trouble is in your own mind."

He would have hit her, but Fear of Consequences held him back. Where on earth was Banley, his wife? Why was she never here when she was wanted? It was all Banley's fault, with her modern theories on parenthood. Why hadn't she controlled the girl? Letting her read all those magazines. Didn't she know what eventual effect they must have on her. Letting her wear a mini-skirt. How provocative! He could almost see the girl's backside every time she bent over.

"What'll you do if I tell you his name?" Marina asked, quietly.

"I shall ask him to call and see me, and quietly suggest to him that you both get married. I'll even marry you myself in the Church!"

"That's sacrilege, or something, isn't it?"

"Don't bother your head about what it is! I can defend my own conscience."

"What if he happens to be married?"

"Oh, my God!" Black despair, ultimate, black despair!

"It was Humphrey Holdeness," she said. She hadn't been out of the house that morning, Banley hadn't been out of the house. They didn't know. He knew, of course, he'd known since the service at eight o'clock. For the first time in a very long time, he felt like praying. The door opened, Banley came in. "Aren't you ever coming for lunch?" she said, "I've got a nice piece of beef from Wilkins and it won't stay good for ever, you know!"

"They don't have a conductor on the London coach, Inspector. An inspector takes the fares before the coach leaves. First stop London, they don't need a conductor. The union played hell of course. We've had a word with the inspector. He can't even remember the carri-cot, let alone what was in it. We've had a word with London. They can't remember the carri-cot either. We've looked in lost property; no carri-cot was handed in," Sergeant Bruton said.

The phone rang. "Aveyard."

"Your Mr Holdeness. No trace of any injury other than the break. He'd had coitus shortly before he died, his stomach shows four pints of beer consumed; he must have been like a camel. He'd eaten baked beans, and a packet of crisps, onion flavour. We can't say exactly when, but not too long before the accident."

"Who said it was an accident?"

"No-one, we just assumed . . ."

"Well don't assume. Don't assume anything!"

"Sorry, Inspector. Just one other thing!"

"Yes, what's that?"

"There appears to be some doubt here about the job number. We've got it down as 4753, but he was labelled 4752/c. Is there a connection with 4752, that jaw-bone job?"

"That's what I'm trying to find out," Aveyard said.

"Well, when you know, will you give us a ring and we'll sort it out? That's most important, you know, to get the right job number."

Sunday morning, just before lunch, the village settles

down. Tuned motor bikes come back from Trial runs, carburettors adjusted to a hair's breadth. The exhaust pipe's strapped on with wire, but that's a job for next Sunday morning. Brian King's back from his walk with Falstaff,a rabbit in his inner poacher's pocket. He had killed it with a stone after Falstaff ran it to exhaustion. There had been a hare, too, but that got into the undergrowth. Arnold Sudbury's pruned his roses, planted a couple of fuchsia slips given to him by Walter Nasset who gets 'em cheap.

"Anything I don't want, you can always have," he says. Sudbury smiles. Doug Minsell's been ploughing the seven acre, praying he won't turn up any bones to set him back a day or two. Sam Gainer's done his accounts, shop and post office; so many forms to fill in his eyes ache, his mind buzzes with figures. Cluney takes the shoulder of lamb bought in Birton out of the oven, red current jelly with it, potatoes cooked in the fat, no vegetables but a green salad 'on the side' the way Sam likes it.

Heather and Roger and Noel Cevicec are already sitting at the table. "What's for dinner?" they're asking. "I'll give you a bucket of worms," Cevicec says. They look out of the window at his garden, but, unlike the rest of the village, they don't laugh. The front garden is a lawn, with a minuscule flower border. All round the lawn bricks are set at the height of the top of the grass. The grass is exactly one inch high, cut every second day in the summer. Every evening, Cevicec goes out with a bucket of Lysol solution, very weak, and sprays it over the grass. Then he stands, and waits, until the worms come up. Cevicec can't stand disorder, can't stand worm casts on his lawn; he fights a daily running battle against them. There's not a weed in his garden, not a worm in his lawn. He picks 'em up and throws them in a bucket. Nobody knows what he does with the bucket of worms after dark, but, when he comes back from his walk, it's always empty. Round the lawn, the bricks are whitewashed. People say locally that you'd better not stand outside Cevicec's house, or before you know what's happened, he'll have whitewashed you, to match the stones around his lawn. Runner beans he plants in military ranks, flowers every twelve inches, no more, no less.

"I wouldn't like to be his missis," Joe Scotia once said in the pub, "I bet he measures and times the strokes."

Cevicec was conscripted into the German Army, gave himself up at Mersah Matruh. He was brought back to prisoner of war camp in England, allowed out to work on farms during the time gap between the end of the war in Europe and Hiroshima. He married a village girl as soon as the war ended, and made a life and a family for himself. In the village in which he had been reared, before the war, women were regarded as common property, less important than the bulls, horses, cows, goats and sheep. These were the natural laws he brought to England with him, laws he observed until the prison camp interpreter caught a girl in a barn with Cevicec and two of his friends. "The law," the interpreter said, "is the law of this land, the customs are the customs here, not where you came from." Whatever Cevicec's instincts had been, he sacrificed them to the laws and customs of the land that gave him a home. It didn't matter to Cevicec that neighbours scoffed at him and his meticulous ways, he was living within the laws of the land. That meant, among other things, that he couldn't take Holdeness outside the pub and thrash him for interfering with Cevicec's wife, and, what's more, he couldn't beat his wife for the same thing. Still, he could beat Holdeness at darts as often as he wanted, and darts was a national pride, wasn't it?

Ingeborg had cooked a Sunday lunch for her father and brother, with two extra portions, one for Bill Aveyard and one for his sergeant. Rolled pork, apple sauce, beans, roast potatoes, apple pie and custard to follow. "Drink beer, do you?" Horst asked. Neither did. "Not when we're working; it makes us sleepy in the afternoon," Aveyard said. Immediately after lunch, Horst and his son Flemming took out the car to go to Chaldwell to look at a stand of oak they'd been promised for cutting. Ingeborg made tea—"You're sure you wouldn't prefer coffee?"—Aveyard would but knew Jim Bruton liked his cup of tea.

"Do you mind if I ask a question," she said, when she'd poured the cups and they were sitting drinking, in that gorgeous post-lunch Sunday euphoria. "Ask away; we don't guarantee there'll be an answer."

"If that bone, you know, the jaw-bone, had been in the ground in the Hall for twenty or more years, how did it happen that Falstaff suddenly dug it up?" She sipped her tea, looked first at Aveyard then at Bruton over the rim of the cup. "It would seem to me that if the ground wasn't disturbed, the bones would settle further down, rather than come to the surface . . ."

Aveyard looked at his sergeant. "Good question," he acknowledged. "Any theories, Sergeant Bruton?" The sergeant thought a while. "The rest of the skeleton was down at about twenty-four inches," he said, remembering. "That's a deep hole for a dog to dig," Ingeborg said, "especially a Labrador that's fed as well as Brian King feeds his dog. A poacher doesn't let his dog get hungry . . ."

"For an obvious reason," Aveyard added; "the poacher wants anything the dog catches for himself!"

The sudden knock on the door startled each of them. Ingeborg answered it, came back into the room almost immediately. "It's your driver," she said, "shall I ask him to come in?"

"We'll go out," Aveyard said. They thanked her for the lunch, went out of the door down the path to where the driver had tactfully waited.

"Mrs Binns," the driver said, "she wants to see you. Mr Binns sent John Scotia up to the police station with a message."

"And interrupted your dinner?"

"No, I'd finished."

"Then wipe the gravy off!"

When Aveyard arrived at the pub, the parson was waiting for him.

"I hope it wasn't inconvenient for *you,* Inspector," he said, "I was just about to start my dinner!"

They went up the stairs together. Nellie Binns was half sitting half lying back in bed. Arthur Binns was standing on the far side of the bed, holding her hand. Her eyes opened as they went into the room. Arthur Binns had draped a woollen shawl round her shoulders, tucked into the neck of the tweed bed jacket she was wearing. He'd combed and brushed her hair, put hair pins in, one of which hung insecurely just above her ear. "This is the Inspector, Nellie," Arthur said.

"Who's the other one?" Her voice was faint with weariness.

"My sergeant," Aveyard said, "but he needn't stay if you don't want him to."

"It's all right. Let him stay. Anyway, you look young to be over him."

"That's what we all say, Mrs Binns," the sergeant said, "but the inspector knows what he's doing."

"Well, if you say so . . ." They all stood about in silence, then, "fetch some chairs, Arthur," she said. The sergeant went with him. There was one armchair beside the bed; Aveyard beckoned for the parson to take it. The sergeant brought in two hard chairs on which he and Aveyard sat where they could look into Mrs Binns' face.

"Mrs Binns insisted I come just as I was," the parson said. Twin spots of red on her cheeks, a last effort, the feeble pulse of energy. "You've got something you want to say to us, Mrs Binns," he urged, gently. Her condition wouldn't last for long. "Arthur wanted to fetch the doctor, but I told him not to bother, didn't I, Arthur?"

"Yes, you did, but I still think he should be called."

"I've got something on my conscience," Nellie said, "and that's where you come in, Parson. But what I've done is wrong, and that's where you come in, young man." Aveyard looked at the parson, who sat in the deep arm chair, fully at ease, his hands clasped.

"The Lord is the final Judge of what's Right and Wrong," he intoned. 'Damn it, he'll be half way through the burial service if we're not careful,' Aveyard thought.

"Whatever's bothering you, Mrs Binns, would you like just to tell us about it," the sergeant said. He'd seen enough terminal cases to know how long the old lady could last.

"There's other people involved," Nellie said, "and I need your promise you'll be kind to them."

"You have that," Aveyard said.

"Justice shall be Tempered with Mercy," the parson added.

"That child you found, the bones, in the grounds of the Hall. I was the one put her there," Nellie said. Poor dying old lady, what a secret to carry to your grave, to have lived with all these years. Aveyard looked at Arthur, standing by the bedside, holding his wife's hand. Frail knotted hands, both of 'em, knuckles gnarled in arthritic age. "Arthur knows," she said, "I've just told him. Poor lad, it's come as a bit of a shock to him, after all these years." She attempted a smile.

"Whose child was it, Mrs Binns?" the sergeant asked. Aveyard was glad to leave it to him. Jim Bruton wouldn't push her, had a depth of wisdom and understanding the younger man lacked.

"Do I have to tell you that?" she asked. The sergeant

looked at the parson; 'come on, man, wake up and do your job!' his look seemed to say. "That's a matter for your conscience, Mrs Binns," the sergeant said, looking at the parson while he spoke. Now the parson had the tips of his fingers together, his lips pursed. Still he didn't speak. "Mr Morris is more qualified to talk about conscience than I am," the sergeant said, *"aren't you, Mr Morris?"* It was as if the sergeant had kicked the parson's shins. "You've come this far Mrs Binns," the parson said, "I think you should Relieve yourself of all your Burdens." 'Prissy bugger', Aveyard thought, 'that's torn it'. "Alas, it's not my burden alone," Nellie Binns said. They'd lost her. He looked at Arthur Binns. No help there. Looked at the parson, back in the contemplation of his finger ends. Suddenly, Aveyard felt Jim Bruton's hand on his arm. What the hell, they were policemen, sworn to a duty to enforce the laws of the land. Dammit, he didn't make the laws, daren't have compassion for those who broke them. "It was a long time ago," Arthur Binns said, almost in a whisper. Sod that, a crime's a crime, the law's for always, not just this week, last week. He stood up. "Mrs Binns," he said, his voice loud in the room, harsh as a naked light bulb, "from what you have just said to me in the presence of witnesses, I have reason to believe you have been an accessory after the fact of a crime. Therefore you may be prosecuted. Do you wish to say anything? You are not obliged to say anything unless you wish to do so, but whatever you do say will be taken down in writing and may be given in evidence." Except for the addition of the word 'do' in the phrase 'whatever you do say', it was the full form of the official caution according to Judges' Rules. The shock was immediate, and apparent. Arthur Binns cringed; the parson sat up in his chair, the colour spots disappeared from Nellie Binns' cheeks. For a moment, Aveyard thought he had gone too far. She had closed her eyes. The parson was shaking his head from side to side, his lips tutting in disapproval. Sergeant Bruton, however, was leaning forward on his chair, looking intently at Nellie Binns' face. Her eyes opened. She looked at Aveyard. "It concerns somebody else," she said, "you'll have to ask them."

"Who?"

"You'll have to ask them!"

"Ask who, Mrs Binns," the sergeant said, his voice kindly. It was a perfect piece of timing. "Ethel Gibbins," she said. "You'll have to ask Ethel."

They left the parson with her, and Arthur. "That'll give John Freeman a start tomorrow," Aveyard said, "which is more than he deserves."

"You had to do it, Inspector. With that damned parson there, we'd never have got anywhere."

"She has a right to the parson. Dammit, Jim, she's dying, and she has a right to make her peace. We can't expect things to be made easy for us."

"Sometimes," the sergeant said, "I think you're about a hundred years old."

They went back to the police station. Joe Verney had a day off at Sergeant Manners' request, and a constable from Welby was doing the rounds. Joe and Mrs Verney had gone to Chaldwell to see her mother; tea and sympathy for a lost holiday, and why don't you get yourself a decent job where you can plan ahead. Verney'd given the sergeant a key to the 'official' part of the combined police station; Mrs Verney had left out a kettle, two cups, tea, sugar and milk. "We've only got the rest of today, Jim," Aveyard said. "The Chief'll pull us off this in the morning; He won't wear us handling an accidental death."

"If that's what it is?"

"What else can it be, on the evidence we've got," Aveyard said. The sergeant was looking through his charts of the investigation, all collated in his neat hand. He made a couple of pencilled notes, scratched his head. Aveyard was watching him. "I'll tell you what," he said, a smile on his face. "Let's play a little game. You write down the three questions you'd most like answered, and I'll do the same, and see what we get?"

"You've read my mind," Jim Bruton said. "That's what I've just been jotting down—three questions I'd like answered." Aveyard took out his pencil, drew a sheet of paper towards him, and wrote. When he had finished, he folded the paper across and handed it to the sergeant. The sergeant tore a page out of his pad and handed it to the inspector. Each opened his paper. "Snap," the sergeant said, and read off the sheet. "One: Miss Cattell's question. Why did the bones come close enough to the surface to be dug up by a dog. Two: why was Mrs Cevicec so emphatic she'd seen Malcolm Minton approaching the bridge about the time Holdeness died his accidental death, and three: where are Mrs Holdeness and her daughter Christine."

"I have a feeling," Aveyard said, "Christine is still in this village. I know it's irrational, but I just have that feeling. I also have a feeling that both that fellow Fran and his paramour Malcolm Minton were lying when they said they'd been playing bezique, and I have a feeling those war-time bones have nothing to do with these present events. Three feelings . . ."

"The Chief would go mad!"

"Luckily he'll never know. Unless you tell him!"

"Me, why would I do a thing like that . . .?" Aveyard knew his sergeant and the Chief Inspector were close; they'd come up in the service together, both were old-line coppers and respected each other for that. A police force is a club, old members, new members, and there's nothing the old members like better than to sit gossiping about the 'new 'uns'. He knew, however, that Jim Bruton respected him, despite his youth, and would tell the Chief so. Old institutions such as the police force resist change; but the whole character of crime was changing, wasn't it, and with it the type of criminal. Most crimes used to be caused by anger, avarice and poverty; criminals were desperate men. Now crime was often committed for frivolous reasons for 'kicks'. With little true poverty about, the 'craftsman' criminal was disappearing. Once a cat burglar could climb a drainpipe, a cracksman spend hours 'feeling' the tumblers of a safe. Now criminals were often impetuous; if they couldn't get in a ground-floor door or window, they didn't bother; if they couldn't cut through a safe door, or carry the safe away, they'd leave it alone. Big crime was organised with as much preparation as a military operation. Petty criminals were often 'nutters', men with no reason for crime other than the vandalistic, ill-disciplined heat of the moment. In such situations, very often the way a policeman felt was just as valuable to him as the clues he could observe; the look on a nutter's face, the smirk that hid his 'you'll never catch me' boast.

"I'm going to take a walk," Aveyard said, "would you stay here in case the telephone goes?"

"You wouldn't be trying to get rid of me, Inspector?" Bruton asked. "Your walk wouldn't be taking you into the grounds of the Hall, to ask a few questions of Mrs Gibbons?"

"What you don't know can't hurt you . . ."

"I know we're off that part of the job. The Chief said so. He'd be very angry to discover we'd ignored his orders."

"Then he mustn't find out!" Aveyard said, smiling.

They came out of the police station together, walked down Church Row, turned into Bent Hill, walked down to the Bridge. Half the village of Bent seemed to be walking in Bent Hill. There were silences as the villagers approached the police officers, then muttered 'good afternoon'. Brian King, out again with his Labrador. "Nice today, isn't it?"

he said. He had a proprietorial interest in the police; after all, hadn't his dog started it all going. They wouldn't be here if it weren't for the dog. "How's it going?" he asked. "Very well." Falstaff appeared to have recognised Aveyard, came over and stood to have his chin tickled, thrusting his muzzle imperiously against Aveyard's shin. Dutifully he bent down and tickled it. Bruton picked up a stick and threw it; the dog bounded after it and Aveyard was able to make good his escape. "Let's go down here," Aveyard said, "and get off this road." They turned right down the embankment beyond the bridge, into the grounds of the Hall. The Village Hall was to the left, the stream to the right, rhododendrons in front. Aveyard walked down the path through the shrubs, out at the other side. Now the lake was to the left, the stream directly in front of them. Beyond the stream was the site of the bones, marked with white tape.

"Stay here," Aveyard said, "but watch what I'm doing." He jumped across the stream, then, suddenly remembering, turned round.

"Lie on the ground," he called to the sergeant. The sergeant did so, then Aveyard continued to the site of the bone find and ducked under the white tape. He bent over the ground where the bones had been. It had been smoothed back again, returfed. He took a pencil from his inside pocket, and stuck it in the ground. He squatted down, put his hands together, stayed still for a few minutes. Then he rose leaving the pencil in the ground, and walked back to where Bruton was lying on the ground, half concealed beneath a rhododendron.

"What did you see?" he asked.

"When you were inside the tapes?"

"Yes."

"I saw you plant something in the ground. It looked like a twig, or it could have been a pencil. Then you knelt down, and put your hands together as if you were praying. You got up again, and came over here." Aveyard nodded. "By the way," the sergeant said, "whatever it was you stuck in the ground, you've left it there, so if it was a pencil, as I suspect . . ."

"You understand what I'm getting at?" Aveyard asked.

"Anybody lying in these bushes could see what someone was doing over there . . ."

"Quod erat demonstrandum. Now, let's assume a few things. Firstly, assume Mrs Gibbins did have something to do with that burial, all those years ago. Let's even assume it was her baby. Each year, and we're still assuming, she came down here on the baby's birthday, and sticks a flower in the ground. . . ."

"That would account for the dead flowers you found . . ."

"That's right. Planted without roots. Now, one year, this year, when she comes down, our dear friend Holdeness is in the bushes, say with Mrs Cevicec. He see Mrs Gibbins, wonders what the hell she's up to. When La Cevicec has returned to her wifely duties, he comes over here and sees the flower stuck in the ground. This bothers him. He's not over endowed with brains, and perhaps it takes him a day or two to decide to investigate further. He comes back here one evening and starts digging. The first thing he finds is part of a jaw-bone. He's so terrified . . ."

"He shoves the jaw-bone back in the ground, not burying it properly, and scarpers . . ."

"Falstaff comes along, finds the new mound of soil Holdeness has dug up, sniffs around in it, and finds the jaw-bone. That would answer Ingeborg . . . Miss Cattell's, question."

"But it still doesn't tell us much about Holdeness's death, does it? Now, what use, if any, would such a man make of such a piece of information. Blackmail, possibly?"

"For what? If it was blackmail, for money, we'd have seen some sign, a gold wrist watch, a car, something he'd buy. He wasn't a lad to hold on to money, was he?"

"I wouldn't have thought so," the sergeant said, "but we'll know more about that after we've had a word with Mrs Gibbins, won't we, Inspector?"

"The Chief wouldn't like that, Sergeant."

"Ah, maybe not, but who's going to tell him?"

They walked round the lake on the south side, came to the drive just by the entrance from Grove Gardens, the main gate. The large oak gate was closed, bolted, and chained, but that didn't trouble them since they were already on the Hall side of it. Together they walked up the drive. Trees to the left of them, ornamental, dark green in the clear light of the summer's early evening. To the right the parkland, lawns with specimen trees once proudly beautiful, now spoiled by dead limbs here and there, fraying the silhouette. The drive swung to the left and they continued up it. Now the Hall was in sight, towering above them, its height amplified by the rise in the drive. It was a clean-lined edifice the stone glowing warm, welcoming. Shutters were at the windows, all except for the window on the ground floor level by the side door. "How would you like to get on your hands and knees and scrub all the floors in that place," the sergeant said.

They left the drive to head for the east corner of the house, the sound of their footsteps lost on the grass. Now the silence of this slumbering dynastic pile suddenly made itself felt, like the presence of a pandora box filled with mystery and evil. "Did you ever read a story by Maupassant called *Le Hor-la*?" Aveyard asked, his voice the merest whisper.

"Can't say I ever did."

"The hor-la, the 'thing from out there'. It was a presence Maupassant felt every night. It came into his room, ate his bread, drank his carafe of wine . . ."

"You think there may be one of them, in there?" The sergeant too was whispering. Both stood still, momentarily unwilling to go further. Ridiculous. Two grown men. A Sunday afternoon in June. Green grass, roses in the gardens, birds in the trees; well, there should be birds in the trees, but if any were there, they were silent. Shuttered windows, chimneys that carried no smoke. An 'hor-la', a thing from *out* there, now *in* there.

"Where do you suppose this Mrs Gibbons hangs out?" Aveyard asked. It was at that moment that both heard the cry.

"Was that a baby?" the sergeant said. Aveyard dashed forward; this was something tangible, something they could come to grips with, and fear fled from him as he went. The sergeant was panting when they got to the side door. Aveyard knocked, raising the enormous hoop and crashing it down against the door. Bruton found an antiquated bell pull, a wooden handle on the end of a length of thin rod. He tugged at it. From deep inside they heard the ring of the bell. The sergeant was just going to pull the handle again when the door opened. Mrs Gibbins stood there, a woman just the other side of fifty if you discounted the prematurely grey hair. She was dressed in a pair of men's jeans, with a zip up the front. On her shoulders she wore a blue canvas sailing smock, smeared with paint. The sleeves were full length, without cuffs, and they too were smeared. On her feet she wore blue canvas bumper shoes, with a thick rubber sole. Only they had been blue, now the colour showed through only by default. One of them had no lace. She was not wearing a wedding ring. She must have weighed twelve stones, stood five feet nine inches high at a guess.

"Like to see my birth mark," she said.

"I'm dreadfully sorry . . ."

"I'm used to it," she said, "everybody hears about the witch who lives in Bent Hall, and when they come up here, what do they find. A rather fat lady, with a twinkle in her eye . . . It must be an awful shock. You must be the two policemen, one of you's an inspector and the other's a sergeant. You're too young to be an inspector," she said to Aveyard, "so I suppose you must be the sergeant." She smiled her disarming smile, held out her hand.

"Sergeant Bruton, ma'am," the sergeant said. Give him half a chance and he'd have bowed. "Oh dear," she said, "I have got it wrong, haven't I?"

She opened the door wide; they took it for an invitation, and went in. They were in a small lobby, with doors opening from it. "Where shall it be," she said, "the gun room, if you're feeling masculine, the morning room if we're formal, the library to ask a lot of questions."

"Have you got a baby here?" Aveyard said, without preamble.

"A baby. Good Lord no, what would I do with a baby?"

"A woman and her daughter are missing in the village, and we're looking for them. They couldn't have got in here without you knowing?"

"I shouldn't think so for a moment," she said, "but why don't we all look together." She led the way, gun room, lined with glass-fronted cupboards, still actually containing guns, the morning room, once elegant, now with the furniture covered by oatmeal-coloured canvas sheets, the servants quarters, butler's pantry, butler's rooms, the drawing room, the ballroom, games room, with its billiards table covered in green leatherette. Every room through which they passed was still fully furnished, except that the furniture was covered in dust sheets, and stacked into piles in the centre of the room. The carpets had all been rolled and folded, and they too were piled in the centre of each room. There were hanging chandeliers, with the dust and cobwebs of twenty years, bracket lamps, wall lamps. In most of them only one or two of the bulbs worked, and many were without bulbs at all. Each room was tightly shuttered, each had the musty smell of a lifetime of dust. There were twenty-seven rooms in all, according to the sergeant's count; two secret staircases, and a secret cupboard which gave access from a small corridor to a major bedroom. "They were realistic when this house was built," Mrs Gibbins explained with her explosive laugh. "The Master of the house had his private staircase that led directly to one of the servant lassy's room; the mistress had her cupboard installed through which the groom, the coachman, or her favourite footman could pass."

"Why couldn't he just use the door?" Aveyard asked.

She laughed again. "Because the Master would have locked it," she said, "before he went up to the servant's room. Sauce for the gander was not sauce for the goose in those days!"

Perhaps the most surprising thing about the house, however, was the condition of the walls and ceiling of every one of the rooms. Each was covered with a vast mural painting in bright primary colours. Every available surface in the House had received its treatment. The large canvasses had been taken down from the walls, painted over, and stacked in piles before she attacked the walls themselves. Her manner of painting was something neither Aveyard nor the sergeant had ever seen before, a phantasmagoria of infinite detail and crude large-scale colour washing. In the ballroom was a mural painting thirty feet long. In the bottom right hand corner a small group of people gathered around a child, lying on what was recognisably straw. The child had Christ-like features, painted with the skill almost of a Dutch master. The grouping around it, Mary, Joseph, the Magi,was all done with care. But, in the background to the manger, ranged across the entire wall, was a gallimaufry of beasts, spirits, phantoms; some were no more than impressions; some had heads three feet in diameter on a body one foot high; a slab of ochre would suddenly become a tooth, dripping with blood, each drop drawn as carefully as a grape in a classic still life. Other sections were crude and childlike faces with the teeth crudely drawn as children draw them, a house, drawn without perspective, smoke oozing from the chimney.

No sign of a child.

When they completed the search, they found themselves in the outer hall again, having just examined the only room of the house that gave sign of occupation, a maid's room just inside the door. In it was a bed, a comfortable arm chair, and piles of books, newspapers, magazines. There too was an electric stove, a kettle, a grill for making toast. "I just can't understand it," Aveyard asked, "if, as you say, all this still belongs to the present Mr Beresford Bent who lives in America, why hasn't he sold it ? Why is all the furniture still here? And who pays the rates, the electric bill, the taxes . . .?"

He was absolutely perplexed. Obviously this was a question she'd been asked many times. "Strange family, the Bents," she said. "Just like jackdaws, always acquiring possessions. But, like all people with the acquisitive urge, they could never bear to part with anything. All the stuff here will stay until the Bent line dies out. Sir Beresford Bent founded with his East India money and left a will that made legal history. He entailed the lot, the house and its entire contents at the time of his death. Not a thing could be sold unless it was proved to Trustees to be damaged beyond repair, broken. His son fought the will and lost. His grandson fought it again, and he lost. In the will it stipulates that nothing, absolutely nothing, must be taken out of the house and sold. You couldn't even sell a knob off a door, and believe me some of them would fetch a good price these days. Where else could you find a house with door knobs three hundred years old? The father of the present Beresford Bent thought he had the answer in 1926 when they started breaking up some of these old trusts—in the legal phrase of the day, and this will show you how lawyers love the language, he hoped he could 'bar his entails behind the curtain with a bare instrument' . . ."

They all laughed, but Aveyard was still mystified.

"The last of the line, the one who lives in America, thought he could *give* it to the National Trust, but they didn't want it without a handsome endowment for upkeep."

"So you get it rent free for life?"

"Yes, and when I die, I don't know what they'll do. I can't see anybody else coming to live here. Every year a solicitor comes from Birton and checks the inventory. I make him a cup of tea. There's hell to pay if he can't find a table or a chair or a cup and saucer that should be here. He was the one told me about 'barring his entails' one year when I'd thrown out a stool that had got wood-worm, without showing it to him first, for him to 'condemn' it. Every year he pays the rates, the water, the electricity, the taxes. He goes away, and I never see him again for a whole year."

"What would happen if the house burned down?"

'That would be that. Finis. It's not insured, how could it be; you couldn't replace it for a million pounds these days. One day there'll be a Bent who has no son, the house will pass to the public trustees, he'll bar the entailment and turn it into a school or a hospital."

"And until that day, you mean to stay?"

She was silent for a long minute. Take a steady look at her, think with her. "After all, you have a good reason for staying, haven't you, Mrs Gibbins?" Drop a stone in a pool, watch the ripples. "There have been tears and breaking hearts for thee, and mine were nothing, had I such to give." Who'd said that? Byron? And then something about "But when I stood beneath the pale green tree which living waves where thou did cease to live . . ." Perhaps there'll be tears; but perhaps there'll be anger. Perhaps there'll be relief. "What do you mean?" she whispered. You only have to say it and you'll crumble the edifice of twenty-odd years. It'd take a world of effort to put in the ground a daughter you'd loved for two years; it'd take courage and strength to live with that knowledge afterwards. Aveyard felt he could understand the paintings; the care and infinite detail were the symptoms of a mother's meticulous love, the wildness, the great gashes and gouts of colours were the despair that, so close beneath the surface, would need occasionally to erupt. What the hell, it was all so long ago, wasn't it? Why bring it back to the surface again. Why take the one thing she had left, a hard-won sanity, the power to keep a close grip on the tormenting expression of remorse. "I only meant you've made a life for yourself here, and Bent's been lucky that you've looked after things for him, prevented the Hall being plundered as it must have been if it had remained empty."

She opened the door for them. Did her hand press his when they shook goodbye? Who could tell? They walked round the angle of the house. Two hundred yards away, Aveyard stopped and turned.

"You didn't mention the skeleton?" the sergeant asked.

"Leave that for Freeman, in the morning."

"I don't blame you. Is she off her head?"

"The paintings: I think they give a clue. I should imagine one minute she's as sane as the next of us and that's when she paints those lovely figure groups, all that fine detail. But the next minute, she's probably as mad as a hatter, wild sweeps of colour, heads of beasts, fangs that drip blood, all that stuff."

"Thank God we found her in a sane mood."

"Wouldn't it drive you potty, living in a place like that?" Now the evening was turning dark, the sky a deep azure. Now the stone of the house glowed with the last deepened rays of the sun, stood out in sharper silhouette. All laughter had gone, barred by entailment. The House should have been turned into a school with hordes of ragging boys, or offices with the clack of busy typewriters, a bridge head for modern industry. Now there was nothing but a mouldering presence, as tangible and evil as fungus. Both Aveyard and the sergeant shivered, and turned to go. Almost as if to mock them, suddenly they again heard that ghastly wailing sound of a child in horrible distress. "It came from that house," Aveyard said, "I'll swear it did!" "That long bottom room, the ball-room?" the sergeant suggested.

"Look, I don't care how you do it," Aveyard said, "but I want that place entirely surrounded by our lads within an hour. We'll go through that place again, brick by brick."

"It'll be difficult, Sunday evening!"

"I don't care if it's impossible, I still want it done. I believe that child is in there. Mrs Gibbins, clever devil, thinks she's put us off by being open and carting us all round the place. Well, she's got another think coming!"

"You might need authority!"

"I'll wait here until you get back. Then I'll have a word with the Chief and he can get me the authority! And if he's not out of his garden by now, that's just his bloody bad luck!"

It took them an hour to muster a search force; detective constables dragged from the television, from supper, from their baths. Detective constables who'd arranged cribbage games, darts matches, an evening of cards with friends. It was the birthday of one; his wife had promised him 'something special'. They assembled along Church Row, down West Lodge Road, across the front of the House, by the rose gardens. And then they moved forward until every part of the Hall was locked tight in view. Several heard the wailing sound as they approached; when they drew near, it stopped. Aveyard made no effort at concealment, led the inside detachment himself up to the door.

Mrs Gibbins opened it again, her hair wild, a glitter in her eye. "Not again," she said, "I'm right in the middle."

"It's Sunday evening, Mrs Gibbins, and it'd take me a couple of hours to get a warrant, but I can get one, make no mistake." The Chief had grumbled, "Try to get her to let you inside voluntary," he said, "use some of that famous charm of yours on her." Henry Martin, 'duty magistrate', loved to make police look silly; he'd delay issuing a warrant while he watched them squirm.

"What is it you want this time," Mrs Gibbins snapped.

"A more thorough search!" To his surprise she drew back from the door. "Search then, but don't ask me to come with you. I'm up to my ears." In her hand she carried a large palette on which were untidy daubs of paint. Sticking from the pocket of her apron was a six-inch distemper brush, whose bristles appeared still wet. Aveyard left her painting a vast mural up the walls of the staircase. He and his men went through the house again, this time measuring walls, looking for hidden recesses, priest holes, cupboards. They found one, hidden under a staircase, a cavity that had been bricked in. "Break into it," Aveyard ordered.

"There'll be hell to pay," the sergeant whispered.

"I don't give a damn with the life of a child at stake."

They brought in hammers, six and ten pound sledges, bolsters to cut the brick. It took five minutes to breach the wall.

"Shouldn't we cut through quietly?" the sergeant asked. "We'd terrify a child with all this noise."

"If there's a child in there," Aveyard said, "she's past being terrified by somebody hammering on a wall, however loud."

The wall cracked under the impact of the ten-pound hammer. "Take it steady," Aveyard commanded. Now they used the bolster and a club hammer, cutting down the crack. Soon they could lift a brick out, then another. A tap and they got a third, then a fourth. "Torch?" Aveyard took it, switched it on, and stuck his head through the hole. He shone the torch round the cavity, brought his head out again.

"You've heard of the skeleton in the closet?" he said.

The sergeant nodded. "Is she in there?"

"The girl isn't."

"But somebody is?"

Aveyard nodded. "Sitting in a corner. Hands and feet chained together, a tall man, or rather, the bones of one. The rats have had the rest of him, God only knows how long ago . . ."

Now at least, they knew why the first Bent had entailed the house and all it contained, a bloody secret he couldn't bare to have exposed during his life time or the life times of his sons to follow.

Aveyard and Bruton walked together down the drive, marched together, so intense was Aveyard's anger. A Veronica was in full bloom by the bottom of the drive, just off to the left. As they marched past, from the depths of the bush it came again, the thin wail. They stopped. The sergeant circled behind the bush, suddenly pounced. From the bush a cat jumped, a Siamese. It went padding up the drive to the Hall, wailing piteously, sounding for all the world like a child in anguish.

"One word, Sergeant Bruton," Aveyard said, "one word about that, back in Birton, and I'll brain you!"

CHAPTER THIRTEEN

Sunday evening in the village, Aveyard and the sergeant walk up the road together. Joe Scotia comes past them in a Land-Rover carrying bales of straw. The pub light's on already, though it can't be really dark in there. You need light to play darts. Rupert Sudbury's washing his father's car in the drive of the bungalow to earn two and six pence for cigarettes. His father doesn't know he smokes. Wilkins sits looking at the empty grate, his kids banished. He knows he'll have to leave this village where he was born and start all over again. Ruined is a relative word; there's money in the bank to go south of London and set up again as a butcher, the only trade he knows. There's money in meat anywhere, that's not the problem. The Wilkins family has had a name for a long time; Phil can remember the time his dad had a yard at the back, one steer butchered and hung, one ready for butchering, one bought but not yet delivered. The gentry used to come from miles, his father's sausages famous throughout the county. That's how he got the factory contract. It became harder and harder to get meat supplies for that many sausages. Round the back door, one Saturday night. Barnacomb, who transported cattle and horses, knew a man in the knackers' yard. Of course, the inspectors inspect, but you can get round that nowadays since so many people want to pay and receive cash to diddle the income tax authorities; half the stuff that went into the knackers was never booked, either in or out. Phil Wilkins paid out his pound notes and fivers and made his sausages by night after Barnacomb had left. They'd be there, first thing in the morning. The police had no powers of arrest, but they'd inform the appropriate authorities in Birton, and a man'd be knocking on the door at seven o'clock. What'd they do to him, a fine, imprisonment? Who could tell these days. Either way, it'd break the kids, Josie, Fred, and Bob. They'd have to leave the schools he'd sent 'em to, move somewhere down south. What a bloody mess; and all because he'd been a bit careless with a bag of bones, a lad had a hungry dog, and a difficult father.

"Sod Robin Gotch and his sodding carpentry!" he said.

"I feel like a man swimming upstream," Aveyard said. "Every so often I catch a log and then find its going downstream with me. We keep finding things, but do you realise, we've not yet found ourselves a crime. Not a crime we can handle. The county authorities will deal with Wilkins, the archeological society will get Mrs Gibbins' skeleton, Freeman will tackle the skull we found in the ground, the coroner will deal with Holdeness, the parson'll get Nellie Binns, and with luck Missing Persons or the Salvation Army'll find Samantha Holdeness and her daughter, safe and sound, in London. And where does that leave us?"

"Right back where we started," the sergeant said, "in Bent."

"You can go off duty if you like," Aveyard suggested. "I'm convinced there really is nothing here!"

"What about you?"

"I thought I'd accept a supper invitation . . ."

"Mr Gainer . . .?"

"Not exactly, though I might pop in there."

"It wouldn't be Miss Cattell?"

"It most certainly would. . . ."

The sergeant grinned. "I wish I was your age," he said, "you wouldn't get a look in!"

Ingeborg had borrowed her father's Rover. "Where shall we go," she asked, when they set off, "out of Bent, I'd imagine . . .?"

Bill Aveyard grunted, settled back in his corner, thinking. She drove easily, down Bent Hill, past the pub and the Green, Sam Gainer's shop, Scotia's farm to the Birton Road. There was the usual Sunday traffic along the road and she had to wait.

"We could go to my place if you wanted," Bill Aveyard said.

"Direct me." "Turn left."

His place was a flat in the top of an old house on the Birton Road itself. Once this had been the opulent part of Birton, the home of leather merchants, shoe manufacturers, tanners. Now they had all moved into the villages surrounding Birton and kept ponies for their children; the houses had all been cut up into flats and maisonettes. His flat had its own entrance at the side of the house, used the gateway put in originally for tradesmen, shielded from the main drive. He got out and opened the gate, she parked the car outside his door. It was a small flat, as flats go, with one bedroom, one sitting room, a kitchen cum dining room, and a bathroom. Since the ceilings were high, however, the flat had a sense of spaciousness. He'd furnished it from the local saleroom, mostly dark wood of a sensible pre-Victorian period, when furniture was light weight and had a touch of elegance. He got the carpets cheap from a 'fetch and carry' store in Birton; the curtains he'd bought made to measure. It all added up to a pleasing, tasteful, if somewhat characterless place to sleep and eat. "You need a housekeeper," she said, eyeing the dust.

"Are you volunteering?" Conversations within conversations, words with specific meaning don't mean what they say. "What would you like to do?" he asked. "Watch the television, listen to records, eat a meal?"

"We don't have to 'do' anything," she said.

"No, we can just sit and talk. I can look at my navel, you can look at yours . . ."

"Or vice versa?"

"I didn't suggest that . . ."

"Are policemen moral?"

"Not specially. They're careful!"

"That's not the same thing."

"No, it's not, is it?"

He sat on the sofa. It wasn't an invitation, but she came and sat beside him, her hands in her lap. "Is a policeman a policeman all the time?" she asked.

"It tends to be that way, us and them, if we don't fight it."

"But you fight it?"

"Sometimes."

"And other times?"

"It's useful."

"In what way?"

"People rarely say what they mean, often don't mean what they say. It's useful to understand that, in one's private life as well as on the job."

"I'm not a virgin," she said. "Do I shock you by saying that?"

"No, you don't shock me. You surprise me, perhaps, but you don't shock me. You have a strong sense of what's real; I wouldn't think you have much to do with the phoney things."

"Because I don't wear make-up?"

"Not exactly; it's more complicated than that. You've obviously looked at yourself with make-up and without it. And I'd say you'd decided you look better without it. That's real. What would be unreal, and unlike you, would be if you wore make-up because everybody else did. If you'd gone to work in an office because everybody else did, or in a shop. That's one of the things I like about you, that you appear to be original in what you do, but not a rebel. I get brassed off with people who rebel, without understanding what they're rebelling against. I think if you did anything like that, you'd know why."

"I'm very flattered," she said.

"No reason to be. Do you like living in Bent?" he asked, obviously to change the subject. You can get lost if you go too far down any one track, without exploring a few others on the way. This girl wasn't to be had for the price of a few kind words.

"I like Bent. I like it less recently. It's changing all the time, you know, and change never seems for the better."

"Cluney once said that to me," he said, "about a village she was living in."

"She was right. Of course people have to have houses, but I can't understand why they don't build all the new houses in one place in the centre of a field somewhere, new roads and drainage, shops, schools and so on, without ruining the character of a village by grafting modern places on to the old. Take our pub. It used to be a popular meeting place for the old village. My dad used to drink his pint, have a natter, come home again. So did all the other men of the village. The ladies rarely went there, except occasionally at the week-end; it was a man's place. When I was small and I needed Dad for anything, I used to go round to the back door and they'd get him. Sometimes he'd buy me a lemonade. But he never goes to the pub now."

"Why not?"

"Because rowdies like Humphrey Holdeness argue politics—not that they understand much about it—and talk about birds and motor cars and football pools."

"That's the modern way."

"Well, if that's the case, my dad doesn't want it. And I don't blame him; I wouldn't stand it."

"But what about the bungalows at the bottom of Bent Hill and Grove Gardens—surely they've brought a few interesting people into the village?"

"Arnold Sudbury? Walter Nasset? Paul Chalmers? I have my own name for them, the two-litre boys," she said, laughing, "two-litre Rovers, Vauxhalls, Fords, anything that's two litres in capacity. Have you ever heard 'em talk? Or been in their bungalows? Well, I'll tell you about one of them, and you'll swear I'm exaggerating. The walls are distempered, not papered. Well, actually they're painted with emulsion paint if we're being strictly accurate. They won't have papers on the wall because it spoils the 'clean lines'. Clean lines, I ask you, in a bungalow." There was a look of contempt on her face. "You're a snob," he said. She flushed. "I do go on a bit, I suppose," she said.

"Don't misunderstand me. I don't mind."

"You ought to! I try not to be intolerant, but it's hard." She touched his hand. "Sorry if I'm being a bore," she said.

"You're not. I like you to speak your mind. What about the women? Surely, they can't be like their husbands . . . ?" "They all contribute to the village, of course; wives run the Women's Institute, the Mother's Union, the Old Folks Charity, because they'd be bored if they didn't. What kind of motive is that, to do something because you'd be bored if you didn't?"

"Does the motive matter?"

"I think it does. All these village societies came together, and were strong, because the people of a village wanted to act and belong together, not because they were bored. A woman in a village is never bored, unless she herself is a boring person. Mrs Scotia, Mrs Minsell, Mrs King, lived in the village all their lives, they're never bored. But you ask 'em to do something of real value, and they'll do it."

"Are they intelligent?"

"Are you trying to say they're country clod hoppers, because if so, then I'm one too. I know we're not smart, we don't go to Stratford and see the plays, or trooping off to London for the sales, but we do a bit of reading, and a bit of thinking, we see the things about us, we understand the country ways. Useless knowledge, I know, when you get into the front room of a bungalow and everybody's talking about how marvellous the scene in the latest play on in London that show's a man's bottom, or books about transvestites, or films about lesbians."

"But those things are part of modern times."

"I know they are, just as Holdeness was part of the modern times, and bred a poor baby and wouldn't care for it, couldn't keep his hands off the parson's daughter, and added his name to the long list of men who've had Mary Cevicec," she said. Are you always a policeman, she'd asked him. "The parson's daughter, that'd be Marina Morris?"

"Yes, and that's a piece of privileged information I've just given you," she said, "Marina's pregnant, and her father's out of his mind . . ."

"May I ask how you know?"

"I clean the brasses in the Church. So does Banley Morris; she's a simple-minded soul, can't keep anything to herself! It'll be all round the village in a day or two. She nearly fainted when I suggested abortion on medical grounds. He's had one child that's not right already; why take a second chance?"

"A third chance, including Cevicec?"

"A fourth or fifth chance, I'll bet, if the truth is known. Some men have an animal attraction for women. He doesn't appeal to me, but I can imagine he did very well for himself."

He put his arm round her shoulders, drew her comfortably along the sofa to him. "What sort of man does appeal to you?" he asked.

She turned her face, looked up at him. "Can't you guess?" she said. "I don't go to everybody's flat the first time of asking!"

"Does this bus stop at Bent?" the lad asked.

"That's what it says on my schedule."

"Are you the lady conductor?"

"Well, I don't know about being a lady but I'm the conductor all right."

"Can you tell me how much the fare is, to Bent?"

"One and two, single, two and two return."

"Oh heck!" The lad opened his hand. Ten-pence.

"That all you've got?" she asked.

"All I have left."

"Come a long way, have you?"

"From Newcastle. I'm off to see me Dad."

"From Newcastle, all that way on your own. How old are you, ten?"

"Yes, ten, how did you know?"

"I didn't, I just guessed. All the way from Newcastle and off to see your Dad with ten-pence. When's the last time you had something to eat then?"

"I'm not hungry. I had a big breakfast."

"'Ere give over, you're breaking me bloody 'eart. Get over to that buffet and get us a couple of them meat pies, and two cups of tea. You do drink tea, don't you? Tell Maggie I'll be across in a minute to pay for 'em, and get stuck in."

He ate both pies. "Come on," she said, "hurry up, we've got a bus to catch."

"I haven't got enough left," he said.

"You'll be all right. If the inspector gets on, I'll pay the extra four-pence for you."

"My Dad'll pay you back!"

"Aye, well last time I had anything to do with Bent, I wasn't able to be much help to 'em because I hadn't kept my eyes open; maybe this'll even up the score a bit." She rang the bell.

Sergeant Bruton was still working. He kidded himself he was having a meal with the Gainers in order to relax, and because his wife was entertaining her widowed sister, but nevertheless, he was working. "We have a strange tolerance in village life," Sam Gainer was saying. "People talk about the permissive society, but rural communities have been permissive in many ways since the development of the village itself. Most villages have always had 'a woman what does', for example. It'd be foolish to call her a prostitute, though she does sometimes accept little gifts. In our village, as you've already discovered, it's Mrs Cevicec, and God bless her, how many young virgin lads she's set on the right tracks we'll never know! Take another modern craze, abortion. People in villages live among animals, they know about reproduction, they know the herbs that make a cow throw a still-born calf, what makes mares sterile. Provided she's not secretive about it, no village woman needs to have an illegitimate child, since there's always someone knows a brew of herbs."

"It's true what he says, Sergeant," Cluney added. She was sitting in a rocking chair, knitting baby things. "It used to be all wool," she said, seeing his glance, "but now its terylene and nylon and stuff that never shrinks."

"You take these new laws about 'consenting adults'," Sam continued, "they've had a pair of consenting adults in this village for the last thirty years. They live together, eat together, and for all I know they sleep together, but everybody in the village, the old village that is, accepts them. We've had a bit of unpleasantness recently with the bungalows, and that lad Holdeness couldn't button his lip, but the old village accepts Fran and MM as if Fran was a man, and MM his younger wife!"

"MM the man, and Fran the woman, more likely," Cluney said.

"It doesn't matter, the fact is we live and let live, we're completely permissive."

"They'd soon be in trouble if they stepped outside the village," the sergeant said. "People like to think they are tolerant of homosexuals, but when they come into contact with 'em, when they start thinking of them as 'queers', and then it's a different story."

"They do move about quite a bit," Sam said. "Fran spends a night away quite often, about once every fortnight I'd say, and he gets letters from all over the place, Newcastle, Formby, Bristol. Funny thing, a lot of young people write to him; you can tell by the handwriting on the envelopes."

"That's the business of Her Majesty's Mail, Sam," Cluney said, reproving, "you ought not to be talking about the letters people get. That's private, that is . . ."

"I wasn't talking about his letters. I was merely saying, they both move about quite a lot. They don't seem to lead such sheltered lives as people would expect."

"How do they earn a living?"

"Malcolm Minton sells feed stuffs around the farms. I gather he's got a few good agencies, and most of his selling is just repeat orders done by telephone. Fran, well he has independent means. His father owned a lot of land Welby way, sold it for housing. Fran got the money when his father died, what there was left of it by that time. His father was quite a lad with bastards all over the County and drank a lot; how he'd time to manage both activities I'll never know; it isn't as if one helps the other!" "More coffee," Cluney asked obviously embarrassed.

"Yes please," the sergeant said. Put it all together, like pieces of a jig-saw, and see what shape it makes. That's what Inspector Aveyard was so good at. Two queers live together, one of them goes away every fortnight and gets letters from young people—is he messing about? Holdeness doesn't like queers and has said something to provoke Sam Gainer's 'button his lip' remark. Everything seemed to come back to Holdeness, didn't it, and, come to think of it, to Fran. Fran it was who had taken Mrs Holdeness to the bus-stop. Mrs Cevicec had seen someone approaching the bridge—"I'd know that pansy walk anywhere," she'd said, but had refused to name a name. They'd assumed she meant Malcolm Minton, but might she not have meant Fran? "Do you mind if I ask you a historical question, Mr Gainer?" he said, when Cluney had brought in the coffee.

"Whisky in that? Or separate?"

"No thank you!" was his automatic answer, but then, "Why not," he said.

"Why not indeed. We drink Irish here, if that's all right?" It was all right. A large glass. The sergeant settled a notch back in his chair. "What's your historical question?" Sam Gainer asked. "Why do you think a man would entail his estate; not nowadays, but three or more hundred years ago?"

"Sir Beresford Bent?"

"That's him."

"That's an interesting question historically," Sam said, "because it doesn't make any sense. Sir Beresford, saving his presence, had made a vast fortune from the East India Company. He was a trader by instinct, and a dedicated one at that. He believed in buying and selling. A lot of such men founded estates when finally they settled down, but not one of 'em could ever lose the instinct. A lot of them became horse dealers of a sort, buying and selling bloodstock; several of them founded several 'estates' before they finally settled on one. I can't for the life of me think why he should prevent his sons from selling out, if they wanted to, and buying something else. After all, he must have known they'd never be short of money."

"Perhaps he was afraid his successors might squander the money?" Cluney suggested.

"They couldn't. A lot of it was in land, all over the world. Even after taxes and death duties, they say young Beresford Bent still has a modest fortune. The money came down the line; the title would have come with it if Old Josiah hadn't been such a funny bugger and renounced it, but even Josiah couldn't renounce the money!"

"Nothing else was entailed,I believe," the sergeant said, "only the Hall and its contents."

"That's what's so strange. A lot of the money and the property was put in trust, but the Hall wasn't. I haven't seen the document, but I understand it's a sraight entailment, and that's why it couldn't be broken by the legislation after the First World War. No, whichever way you look at it, there's something strange about it . . ."

"It's almost as if," Cluney said, "he wanted to make certain nobody would ever pull down that house."

"As if there was a skeleton hidden beneath the stairs?" the sergeant prompted.

"That's right," she said, "as if there were a skeleton!"

"A blot on the Bent escutcheon, what a flight of fancy," Sam Gainer said, laughing. "Have another whisky and tell us how young Aveyard's getting on. In the police force, I mean!"

* * *

Young Aveyard, to judge by masculine, sensual, physical standards, was getting on very well, and neither he nor Ingeborg Cattell was talking. Dusk had turned to evening, the sky was dark, the room was dark. Sense of touch is heightened in the dark, making love a matter of stroking, caressing. Her lips moved beneath his. He pushed her hair back from her ears, his hand behind her neck, and pulled her to him as they kissed. They were lying on the sofa, all limbs entwined. Love's a physical thing first these days, romance and understanding come later. It's a challenge, a statement, "I want you as much as you want me," an affirmation of separate identity, "I am a man, you are a woman." The needs come later, dependencies, encroachments some can welcome. "The bed's more comfortable," he said. She held up her arms, he picked her up, and carried her into the bedroom, began to undress her with infinite care. The door bell rang.

"Ignore it," he said. It rang again. One, two, then a long one, one two then a long one repeated, the morse code for 'A'.

"That's Jim bloody Bruton," he said, "my sodding sergeant!"

"Your telephone's out of order," the sergeant said when Aveyard let him in. The earpiece had been removed, and one of the leads disconnected. "I'm off duty," Aveyard said. "Not according to the Chief. Two kids, pear-pinching, ruined my supper by finding Marina Morris under the deadly nightshade. And this time, it's not suicide, nor accidental death."

Looking at the body as the forensic men swarmed all around, Aveyard realised what the sergeant meant. The bruises made by her assailant could clearly be seen on Marina's throat.

CHAPTER FOURTEEN

"Whoever did it," the pathologist had said, "is either a strong male, or an angry weak male."

"Or a very angry female?" the sergeant had suggested. That earned him a scowl. "Yes, I suppose so," the pathologist conceded, "a very very angry female."

All the males, and all the females, strong or weak, but certainly angry were in bed when the police squad, hastily gathered, did the rounds of the village. Even Ingeborg had managed to get home in time, though Aveyard tactfully—or was it remorsefully?—left the search and investigation of the wood-yard to the sergeant.

"You see the difficulty, don't you, Inspector," Bruton said, "we know Miss Cattell was out, but by the time we came to question them, she was back, and neither her brother nor her father could say what time she came in. The same could be true for whoever murdered that girl; they could have been out, and even the people in their homes might not have known what time they came in."

The parson was sitting in the deep armchair in the library when the inspector went to interview him, staring into an infinite space.

"How much did you know about your daughter's private life?" Aveyard asked, kindly. He'd just had a first report from the pathologist over the telephone.

"Not enough, Inspector," the parson said.

Banley Morris came into the library with two cups of coffee.

"You won't sleep anyway," she said to her husband as she handed him a cup. She'd put sugar in the cup she gave to the inspector, but he said nothing about it, other than to murmur thanks and ask her to stay. "I was asking Mr Morris how much you knew about the private life of your daughter," he said, when she had settled in a chair. She looked at her husband. "I told the inspector we didn't know enough," he said. Weak men either harden at moments of crisis, or dissolve in their own salt tears; it was too soon to judge which would happen to the parson.

"When we discover a young girl is involved in a crime," Aveyard said, "there are certain tests we always carry out as a matter of routine . . ."

"We knew she was pregnant," her mother said.

The parson shook his head at the blunt directness of her words.

"Yes, that's what we'd discovered. It would help if you could tell us who the father was?"

"We don't know, Inspector," she said.

"Or might have been? Were there any steady boy-friends?"

Again the parson shook his head. "She didn't seem to be much interested in young men. That's what was so astounding about her . . . condition. She was such a quiet young girl, more, sort of, well, she wasn't the sort of girl to be gadding about with young men, if you know what I mean . . . ?"

Aveyard was listening to the words, but watching Mrs Morris' expression. Lips tightened, eyes flashing scorn until she realised she was being observed, then she looked down into her lap, her hands clenched. A father is the last person you should ask about his daughter, if you're concerned to know what the daughter was like. "Who were her friends, Mr Morris?" he asked.

"You could try that Sudbury boy, or the twins Cheryl and Amanda . . ." No mention of the Holdeness man, who's dead now. If the girl would consent to go with Holdeness, her standards couldn't get much lower.

Shock tactics; since there's a crust of complacency on them as thick as cream curd. "I believe she knew the man Holdeness rather well?" Aveyard asked.

"She knew everybody in the village *rather well*, if it comes to that. You seem to forget, Inspector, I have a position here: naturally, as my daughter she was someone of consequence. She was a good girl, Inspector, and the village people looked up to her, and respected . . ."

"Pregnancy isn't always caused by respect, Mr Morris. It's caused by knowing people well enough to be intimate with them. I'm not concerned about your daughter, or the state of her morals. Someone has committed a crime by killing her, and that's the person I'm after. Incidentally, someone also committed a crime by having intimate relationships with her before her sixteenth birthday, but that's a different matter. It's tempting, though not necessarily logical, to think they may have been the same person. That's why I want to know who were her friends. I shall find out, Mr Morris, with or without your help; believe me I shall soon know more about your daughter than you or your wife apparently knew!"

It was brutal, but it worked; at the crisis, Mr Morris became, as Aveyard hoped he would, a strong man. "I had to reprimand Marina," he said, "for keeping company with that chap Holdeness; she promised me she would never converse with him again. She also knew the man Cevicec rather more than I wanted—we had him here to attend to the garden from time to time and once I caught them skylarking about."

"What were they doing, Mr Morris?"

"I don't know, exactly, but they were giggling and laughing at the top of the lawn behind the bushes; I tried to get up there quietly to observe them, but they must have seen me coming, or heard me. I've never had him to do the garden since."

"Anyone else?"

"There was one boy. I never knew who he was. I tried to catch him twice, but missed him."

"Catch him? Where was he?"

"In the drive way, just inside the gate. Both times he heard me coming, and ran. Marina said she'd been taking a walk on her own, but I knew she sometimes lied to me."

"What were they doing, just inside the gate?"

He looked at his wife, but she could give him no guidance. "They were kissing," he said, "or at least they were standing very close together, and I imagine they were kissing."

"And you never knew who he was?"

The parson shook his head.

"Was he someone from the village?"

"I never caught more than a glimpse of him. He could have been anyone, so far as I know."

"Did you ever find anything among Marina's possessions, Mrs Morris; any notes, or letters, any small gifts?"

She shook her head. "I think you ought to tell the Inspector, Banley," the parson said. Again she shook her head. Some things a woman cannot bring herself to speak about.

"Once we found, in the drawer in Marina's room, a . . ." He stopped. Aveyard waited. Memory's like polish stain you rub on loved wood to hide the scratches and make it shine; the mind selects, suppresses, edits, rearranges, even reshapes, events and characteristics. How often had people said to him, 'she was a good girl, my girl was'; or 'our Dad was a good man'; or 'our Mam would never do a thing like that'.

"It's a terrible way to kill someone, Mr Morris, to strangle them to death. Whoever does that once, could do it again."

"She had a packet of contraceptives," he said, "the kind of thing they sell for men. I burned them." He bent his head forward, lifted his hand to cradle his forehead, and wept. Were those contraceptives bought to prevent his daughter becoming pregnant. Had he, inadvertently, been responsible for her pregnancy?

"Anything else you found, anything?"

The parson shook his head.

"Mrs Morris, anything *you* found. Anything at all out of the ordinary . . . ?"

"She had a man's tie once, in her handbag. She said they'd taken it from one of the young boys, for a bit of a lark. I made her give it back."

"A school tie, was it?"

"No, I've never seen one like it before. At first, I didn't know it was a tie."

"Why not?"

"I'd never seen one like it before. I made her give it back, but she never said where she'd got it. Sky-larking about, I suppose."

"Why didn't you know it was a tie, Mrs Morris?"

Patience, patience, let her tell it her own way.

"Because I've never seen one like it before. It was made of green suede leather! Have you ever seen a tie made of suede leather, Inspector?"

Yes, he had. Hipster trousers, hair slicked down, a striped shirt in purple, pink and mauve, yellow boots, and a green suede leather tie; it was Flemming's Saturday Night with-it gear, just the sort of outfit to appeal to a susceptible young girl who's spent her life seeing her father in a dog collar, and her mother in a twin set and pearls; a young girl who's been fed 'Thou shalt not' with porridge every morning.

It was breakfast time; Ingeborg cracked another egg into the pan as she saw Aveyard coming up the path, through the wood-yard. "Working," she asked, when she opened the door. He nodded. "Flemming?" "I'm afraid so; is he in?" She beckoned him inside, shouted up the stairs. Flemming came clattering down, as if he'd been waiting at the top. In his hand he held the diesel engine key, fondling it nervously.

Cevicec had just arrived home from work. "Take the sergeant into the front room," his wife said. "I'll bring you some tea." "Not when I'm working, Mrs Cevicec!" "Why not?" Yes, indeed, why not? "All right, then!" "Take sugar?" "Yes please, two spoonsful." "Makes you fat!"

Sergeant Bruton waited until she'd come with the tea and gone again before he spoke.

"I believe you know, or rather you knew, Marina Morris quite well?" Save the royal police 'we' for later, when there's a need to invoke the majesty of the law. Keep it first person singular, inspires confidence and, you hope, confidences.

"Yes." East Europeans; what do you do, get out the cosh and slip into your polished jack-boots.

"Rather better than most people?"

"I had her a time or two, if that's what you're getting at."

And there it was, just like that. 'I had her a time or two'.

"You know it's an offence to have carnal knowledge of a girl under sixteen in this country, Mr Cevicec?"

"Yes, I know. But it's only my word, isn't it? Look, Sergeant, people don't account me very much; they laugh at me because I like things neat and tidy, and because I speak with a funny voice, and because, well, you know about my wife and other fellahs; but when Cevicec wants, he can be as good as the best of 'em. That's Cevicec for you."

Open the tin lid, watch the maggots squirm, then go fishing. "They didn't treat you right, Mr Cevicec."

"You don't keep Cevicec down, Sergeant! What did I care what they were saying?" Cevicec reached inside his pocket, drew out a post-office bank book. "There it is, Sergeant, and I don't owe anybody a penny. Cevicec pays his way! Cevicec pays everybody!"

"Just as you paid the parson . . . ?"

"I had his daughter, anytime I wanted, and you can't get much better in a village than the parson's daughter."

"And what about Holdeness; you paid him too?"

"You think I pushed him over the bridge?" Cevicec laughed. "I wouldn't do a thing like that, anymore than I'd put my hands round Marina's throat and strangle her. Cevicec knows what he's doing!"

"He's out of his mind, Inspector! I tell you, he's out of his mind. The Great Cevicec. Nobody can do Cevicec down and get away with it. The parson treats him a bit off-handed, Cevicec takes offence, and decides to get his own back by deflowering the parson's daughter; the only thing the Great Cevicec doesn't know is that Holdeness, and others I wouldn't be surprised, have already deflowered her. Holdeness messes about with Cevicec's wife, and what does Cevicec do? He gets his revenge, by putting sand in the tractor gearbox, dumping his bucket of worms on

Holdeness's lawn, practising darts until he knows he can beat Holdeness in the pub, giving Holdeness bottles of port and vermouth in which he's urinated! I thought the ways of we British were sometimes a little odd; if this is the East European mind in action, thank god for the Iron Curtain."

Bill Aveyard had never seen Jim Bruton so perplexed.

"All right, Jim," he said, "let me ask you one question." First name used, no rank, therefore the question and its answer are both unofficial. Each knew that. "You've seen Cevicec in action, you've talked with him, you must have formed a personal opinion. Did he strangle the girl?"

Jim Bruton hesitated, thought again about Cevicec as he last saw and heard him. "No, I'd say not," he said finally.

"Why not?"

"You know the expression, can't see the wood for the trees? I should think Cevicec's like that. You know I'm not much on psychology—I leave all that sort of stuff to you—but I would say that Cevicec's too concerned with the little things to go for the big ones. Any other man would have given Holdeness a damned good hiding, and Mary Cevicec too, come to that. But Cevicec's not like that—though I grant you he's strong enough to do it, and rough enough. But his way is the sly way; he has a narrow view of things, a little ugly twisted narrow view."

"You don't think he could have lost his temper, and put his hands round her throat. You don't think she might have provoked him? Taunted him, maybe?"

"I don't think he's the sort of man ever to lose his temper in ways we know. He'd never strike out. It'd be like a cancer growing inside him. I'm sure he's got an enormous grudge against the world, because he's a foreigner, and 'talks funny', because he's very meticulous in the way he does things. But surely, the very fact of him being so meticulous means he's incapable of the big business of losing his temper. No, I don't think he did it. I think that no matter how much she might have provoked him, his answer would have been small, petty, mean, sly."

Aveyard had names on a sheet of paper in his notebook. He ringed the name of Cevicec.

"What about young Cattell?" the sergeant asked.

"A possible. Once again it rears its ugly head!"

"Sex?"

"Sex, and what passes among the young people for love; love and sex, they've become interchangeable."

"How old are you, Bill?"

"At moments like these I feel a hundred and five! Flemming Cattell is attracted by Marina Morris. Fancies her. Takes her out a time or two; he was the one the parson spotted by the front gate. They were, to quote Flemming, just fooling around."

"It used to be called, 'grabbing a feel!'"

"The extent of your knowledge constantly horrifies me . . !"

"Me too. Did he know about Holdeness? Or Cevicec?"

"He knew there'd been others. Suspected Holdeness and Cevicec. He followed her a couple of times when he knew she had a date, but she spotted him, apparently, and lost him."

"Has he got a temper?"

"Hard to say. He's direct-in-line Scandinavian stock; he appears to be slow moving, slow thinking. He's not very bright, but who the hell knows what's inside, what he's capable of if he's roused. He followed her; it's a small thing, but it takes a special kind of mind to follow another person."

"Don't I know it; I never feel comfortable. As if I'm peeping through curtains at a woman taking a bath."

"It's here, somewhere, Jim. And I get the feeling we're not going to find it by ordinary means. The path. department is no help to us at all. Too many footprints where she was found, bruises on her throat, certainly, but any two of a hundred thumbs could have made them."

"We need a Sherlock Holmes to say he was a left-handed pygmy of Anglo-Iranian descent with a squint in his right eye . . ."

"Any suggestions?"

"She was pregnant, and some fellow strangles her, in the place they meet, without having intercourse with her, without assaulting the body alive or dead. Suggests to me, Bill, that they'd met by appointment, and that she was giving the man an ultimatum. 'You've got me pregnant, now get me out of it,' or 'you've got me pregnant, now marry me . . .'"

"If he was free to marry her!"

"Which is unlikely. Anyway, she wasn't sixteen." Both the sergeant and the inspector lapsed into silence. Thinking. Thinking. An investigation has a technique; there are rules you follow, methods. Birton had all the mechanical aids required, but this time, nothing! Of course, they might turn up a hair, one hair, in the girl's clothing, a formal 'clue' that can be interpreted by forensic skill. But what happens when there are no clues. Two people meet by appointment; they don't have to touch each other. They argue. The man stretches out his hands, places them around the girl's neck, and squeezes. She falls to the ground, dead. Dammit, it could happen that the only parts of him to touch her are the palms of his hands. Dammit, he could even be wearing gloves, though that's unlikely. Motive? Simple. The girl's pregnant, and she's under age. The man who made her pregnant not only faces all the consequences of the actual fact of pregnancy, he also faces criminal charges for having had 'carnal knowledge' of her. The minds of the inspector, and of the sergeant, for once were in parallel. "Strangling's a hate thing," Aveyard said.

"I was just asking myself why it was a strangling, and not a blow, or a blunt instrument?"

"Strangling builds up from hate. Whoever it was, he went there hating her for what she could do to him. Probably for what she was threatening to do to him. Putting his hands round her throat might just have been to stop her talking, stop her saying those terrible things a girl would say at such a moment . . ."

"Like, 'I'll tell your wife'?"

"Like anything that'd ruin him."

"You know, Inspector," the sergeant said, going back on duty, "I think we may have been approaching this from the wrong angle. We've been looking at the people we know she knew, and none of them has much to lose. Flemming would get away with a 'carnal knowledge' charge on a plea he thought she was over sixteen; Cevicec wouldn't be worried by such a charge. We want to look for a married man, who appears respectable, who's got a lot to lose, and who's got a wandering eye."

"The bungalows?"

The sergeant nodded.

Sam Gainer was sitting behind the counter of his empty shop. The murder of Marina Morris had shocked him, taken his mind back to another young girl murder in another village.

"Seems to follow me and Cluney about!" he said, "violence, murder!"

"You've got to help me," Aveyard insisted.

"I can't, Bill, I truly can't. I can't go on thinking about these things. All I want is a quiet life, with Cluney, and the baby when it comes, and the shop."

"That's my job, Sam, to make it more possible for people like you to enjoy a quiet life, with your wives, and your kids, and your jobs and businesses. But you have to help me!" Cluney came in from the kitchen with the routine cup of coffee. Bill Aveyard took it from her, put it down on the table, and forgot it. The sergeant sipped his, secure in his years of experience. He's travelled this route before. Thinking men think themselves soiled by an exposure, however remotely, to the sordid facts of a crime. Thinking men refuse to accept the depths to which the human ethos can sink. 'How can they do that?' they ask, but it's a futile question. Bruton knew, and Aveyard eventually would come to know, for it was the nature of their job, that the human mind has been created with an infinite capacity for evil and good, in equal amounts, and though the good men do is often transcendental, the evil can wallow hog-like in inconceivable mire.

"I think I might be able to help you," Cluney said.

"Oh Cluney, stop it!" Sam Gainer said.

"If I heard your question right," she persisted, "you're interested in the bungalows. Well, I probably know as much about them as Sam does, so ask me!"

"Won't you be quiet, woman?" Sam asked, gruffly.

"No, I won't, Sam," she said. "We're going to have a baby, and that baby could be a girl. No, I won't be quiet."

Sam sat there, defeated by her logic. Aveyard saw Sam wouldn't interfere, glanced at Bruton, who had a notebook and pencil ready.

"Of all the people in the bungalows, give me the names of the men who might lose their temper."

Cluney thought for a while. "Walter Nasset, of course, he's got a vile temper. He's known for it. Barden's a bit of a curmudgeon, Arnold Sudbury's kids are afraid of him, Bailey flies off the handle occasionally, but he works too hard and his wife's a bitch, and he has good reason to. Thompson, perhaps, no, I don't think Thompson would ever lose his temper sufficiently to strangle a girl . . ."

"Don't think about that," Aveyard cautioned, "just think about men who qualify to each of the questions I ask, without speculating if they could or could not be a murderer!" He looked at the sergeant; he had not crossed off Thompson's name. "Anybody else?" Aveyard asked.

"No, I don't think so. They're a pretty innocuous lot, really. Bank clerks, solicitors offices, play the recorder, sing in the Choral Society, do no evil, hear no evil, speak no evil . . ."

"And do no bloody good either!" Sam interjected.

"Next question. And this is difficult. Give me the names of the men who either have, or think they have, a social position. Men who are a bit, say, pretentious, socially."

"That's easy," Cluney said. "There's a little clique, vying with each other to have the best cars, to give the best parties, to go to the furthest point for their annual holidays. Is that the sort of thing you mean?"

"Kids never seen out on the street scruffy, men who let you know the job they have, or the business they run, is impressive."

"Three of 'em. Bailey, Nasset, and Sudbury. That's all. The rest are quiet people, who do no entertaining, don't mind buying margarine here in the shops. Nasset's wife would die rather than admit to having margarine in the house. Bailey lets you know the cost of everything in ordinary conversation, Sudbury was sneering about Majorca, saying they go to Minorca."

"And don't speak a bloody word of Spanish!" Sam said.

Bill Aveyard didn't quite know how to phrase the next question; he looked at the sergeant for guidance. The sergeant cleared his throat. "Can you tell me, Mrs Gainer, how many of the men are unfaithful to their wives . . . ?"

She answered instantly. "They all are," she said, "in the mind if not in the flesh. 'Packet of cigarettes, Mrs Gainer, and my, aren't you looking attractive this morning.' You'd be surprised!"

The sergeant looked back at Aveyard. Ball's back in your court, Inspector, he seemed to say.

"How many would you think have done anything about it, actually been physically involved with another woman?"

Cluney couldn't guess at that, of course. "Secretaries," she said, "girls in the office. You can't really tell, can you, these days?"

Sam reached out, tore a page from the book in front of him, wrote a name on it, and handed it to the inspector. "That's it, Bill," he said. "I'm sorry, but there's a limit, for me, and for Cluney. No, don't read that in here. It's all talk with most of them. It's all in the mind. There's only one of 'em, if it really came to it, who'd have the nerve to do anything about it, and that's his name. But don't read it in here, and don't ask us any more questions."

Without a word, the inspector and the sergeant got up, and left. Aveyard held the folded paper in his hand.

"He'd have to meet her in the first place," the sergeant said, "and it's not easy to turn a casual 'how do you do' into an intimate situation. It'd be easier if he had kids of his own, in a sense. That'd get her inside his house. 'They're out at the moment, Marina, but why don't you come in and wait. They won't be long. They've gone to the shops with their Mother.' Once inside, of course, anything could happen. So many girls these days, blast it, seem to prefer men old enough to be their father."

Aveyard opened the page of the note-book, looked at the sergeant. "Sudbury," said Bruton, "for five bob."

Aveyard nodded.

"I've been expecting you," Arnold Sudbury said, "but

not so quickly. It wasn't my kid, I'm certain of that, but she was going to say it was. There's been lots of others, she was a nympho, you know, but I suppose I was the only one who had a bit of money. She wanted me to take her away. Give everything up and take her somewhere sunny, that's what she said. I've got a life here, a business, a lot of friends. I couldn't give it all up for a fifteen-year-old nympho who was having a kid that wasn't mine. She wouldn't have an abortion. That's when I lost my temper. I never really cared about her, I mean, she was just there, available. *She* was the one started it. If you get down to it, I suppose, really, I hated her!"

Aveyard and the sergeant went back into the shop. "It was Sudbury," Aveyard told Sam. Sam nodded, not surprised. "Sorry I sounded off a bit, but I really do believe a child can be affected by its mother's thoughts. Come and have that supper you never finished last night," he said to the sergeant, placating.

"I'd love to," Jim Bruton said. He felt he owed Sam Gainer that much, and his wife still had her widowed sister with her.

"Will you come too?" Sam asked.

Aveyard didn't reply. Ingeborg had just come into the shop.

It was half past eight by the time he'd finished wrapping up the case. He'd given her the key to his flat, and took in a paper of fish-and-chips. She was waiting for him, in bed, and he made the mistake of eating the fish and chips first. "Not again," he said, as the doorbell rang its 'A'. The sergeant had brought a boy with him, a tall-for-his-age lad of ten. "He stopped me on my way out of Sam's," the sergeant explained. "He's travelled from Newcastle, on his own, to look for his dad."

"Where does his dad live?" Aveyard asked.

"In Bent, of course, but in a house called Tolly's!"

CHAPTER FIFTEEN

The Newcastle police were efficient. Within thirty minutes of Aveyard ringing them, they phoned him back with the story. "The boy's name is said to be Richard Francis. He lives at number 15 Marlborough Way, a street of better class semi-detached houses in a good suburb. His foster parents are Mr and Mrs Ellison, Mr Ellison is the manager of a shoe shop, Mrs Ellison doesn't go out to work. They have no children of their own. They never thought of adopting a child until, nearly ten years ago, a man appeared at the house with a newly born baby in great distress, or so it seemed. He said he'd been given their name by a mutual friend, but when pressed, he wouldn't identify anyone. He said his wife had just died, that he was incapable of bringing up the child, and would they take the child in, as foster parents. They demurred at first, but then he produced a hundred pounds, said he'd pay them four hundred pounds a year to bring up the boy, quarterly in advance, and they decided to do it. He's been back to see the boy at least once a quarter, there's never been any delay about the money, he's always given them twenty-five pounds at Christmas to buy 'something extra', and they've rather taken to him. The boy's been getting a bit independent recently, hard to handle. They had to reprimand him on Saturday for answering back, and Sunday morning, when they came down for breakfast, they found the boy missing. They didn't report it to the police or phone the father expecting the boy would turn up sometime during the day. They recognised the boy's father from the description you gave. They'd be pleased to have the boy back; they seem genuinely fond of him."

"Fran, fathering a boy?" the sergeant said to Aveyard, "he's as queer as an old boot. Ten years ago, he must have been pushing fifty, and we know he's been living with Malcolm Minton all that time."

"Being queer is a thing of the mind, Jim," Aveyard reminded him, "many a queer gets married and fathers a family, if only to divert suspicion." Still he was bound to agree with Bruton; he just couldn't see Fran in the role of a father. He telephoned to Sam Gainer. "Secrets of Her Majesty's Mail, Sam?"

"What do you want, but don't for God's sake let Cluney know!"

"Unofficially, of course!"

"Of course!"

"These letters Fran gets from all over the country. Can you remember off-hand if one of them comes from Newcastle?"

"Yes, regular as clockwork, each Monday morning, one from Newcastle, and one from Bristol. There's one from Liverpool, not quite so regular, and one from Sittingbourne."

"I don't suppose any of 'em has a return address?"

"The one from Sittingbourne has. Classy envelope, always, and I remember the place, a lovely Anglo-Saxon name of Bredgar. Pear Tree Cottage, Bredgar, Nr. Sittingbourne."

"I owe you an Irish for that!"

The Bredgar policeman was able to confirm the same story. "We're very close here, you know. About eight years ago, the Blakeleys took in a little boy, Martin was his name. I sometimes see the father when he comes to visit. I was the one gave him their name in the first place, after his wife had died. Of course, it's not part of the official adoption scheme, but the couple's fairly well-to-do, and they fairly worship that boy, and the father was very distressed when he came here first with the baby. I don't know what they'll do if the father ever claims him; apart from anything else the money must be quite handy. I understand they get a hundred pounds a quarter, payable in advance, always on the dot." Village lives, village interconnection. Everybody knows everything. But why had there been no whisper in Bent of Fran's wife? To judge from the letters she'd borne him four children, and he'd boarded them out all over the country, always with the same story, "I can't bring up the child on my own now my dearly beloved wife has died!" It was a story and a scene to catch any woman's heart. Easy to do, take the child with you to some strange town, find a good-looking suburb, ask a few questions in the local shops, about married couples with no children, old enough not to have children of their own. Four hundred a year would tempt anyone, especially with a lovable child and a distraught father to seal the bargain. Plus the sight of a hundred pounds. It must be costing Fran a fortune but then, he could afford it. And that would be where he went each time he left Bent; he'd be visiting one of his sons.

But why the elaborate deception?

Why?

* * *

Ingeborg had modestly stayed in the bedroom. She pouted when Aveyard came in, shut the door behind him. "I thought you'd forgotten me?" she said. "Can you help me?" he asked. She could detect the note of urgency in his voice. "Of course," she said, and leaped out of bed quite unself-consciously. Aveyard felt a momentary pang of regret as he saw her naked figure, but he spoke to her while she got dressed again. "There's a boy out there," he said, "and I want you to look after him for me. Do you think you could ring your father and get his okay to stay here with the boy if necessary?"

"I don't need to ask his permission," she said, "not at my age; but I'll ring him a bit later on, just for courtesy, and let him know I shan't be home."

"Second thing," he said, "can you think of any woman in Bent who might have had four children during the last ten years and kept them a secret from everybody?"

She had no need to think for long. "Impossible," she said, "I know everybody in Bent and believe me, no-one who could have hidden a thing like that. Who's the father?"

"It could be Fran!"

"Fran?" she asked, incredulous. "You must be joking. I mean, he's not capable; well, I've no proof of that, but I thought . . ."

"That's a common mistake to assume a homosexual can't become a father, but its not true."

"But it's entirely out of character for Fran. He's nervous of women, he's shy, except of Malcolm Minton. No, rely on my female intuition, but I just can't see Fran climbing into bed with a woman, with any woman . . ."

"Malcolm Minton, then?" Wild thought.

"Same again, exactly the same again. Anyway, Malcolm's like a woman himself. He's got all our worse qualities, with none of our virtues. He's waspish, vindictive, petty, he's well at home with women, I'll grant you that, but I can't see him in the act."

She had dressed herself. The sergeant, bless him, showed no sign of surprise when she came out of the bedroom. She took to the boy instantly. "You must be hungry," she said, "if you've come all the way from Newcastle; let's go into the kitchen and see what we can find!"

She led the boy away. "The female point of view," Aveyard grinned, "feed 'em first, ask questions later."

"It makes good sense; maybe we should carry haversack rations with us to hand out to people we want to question."

"What have we got, Sergeant?" Aveyard asked. Jim Bruton noted the use of rank. It made a useful indicator; he was Jim when they were off-duty, Sergeant when there was work. "Miss Cattell is convinced Fran couldn't be the father of those children, and yet he behaves like a father, spends money for their upkeep, visits them, has them call him 'Dad'."

"How's your mathematics, Inspector?" the sergeant said.

"Fair, only fair."

"Richard here is ten, Martin in Bredgar is eight. We think there are four of 'em, so let's make a mathematical progression and say one of the four would be six years old, the other four years old. If there was to be a fifth . . ."

"It'd be two years old?" Aveyard thought deeply. "No, Sergeant, it's too impossible. Anyway, Christine is a girl . . ."

"We don't know what the other two are, in Liverpool and Bristol. They could be girls . . ."

"They could be. Anyway, we both seem agreed that, wherever he gets the children, Fran is a very unlikely natural father for them. It's also strange, and therefore perhaps significant, that his 'children' are lodged as far apart as Newcastle, Liverpool, Bristol and Sittingbourne. They couldn't be further apart!"

"But he's at the centre of them all, here in the Midlands."

"But why, Sergeant, why? And where does he get the children?"

"I suggest we ask him," Bruton said.

Aveyard had a book of maps of England on his shelf. He took it out, opened it at the complete picture of England on one page. He drew pencil rings round the four towns where Fran had children, drew a ring round the approximate location of Bent. "Assuming you wanted maximum spread, assuming you had to pick one more town, assuming it had to be somewhere you get to and from quite easily, where would you pick?" Bruton looked at the map. Aveyard handed him the pencil, nodded when the sergeant touched the map with it. "Norwich," he said, "that's where I would pick!" He took the telephone, dialled, spoke to the duty officer at Birton police headquarters for a couple of minutes. "It's a long shot," he said, "but worth trying."

Fran was in the sitting room with Malcolm Minton when Aveyard and the sergeant arrived at Tolly's. Aveyard had a photograph he'd taken with a polaroid instant developing camera. They had been playing draughts together, and the counters were still on the board on the table. This was the first time Aveyard had been inside their home! It was exquisitely furnished and decorated, a showpiece that reflected that quiet taste and wealth of its occupants. Nothing was out of place, there was not a trace of dust on any surface, no grubby fingermarks, no stains on the carpet where children had dropped cups of cocoa, no hurriedly misplaced work baskets dumped when a harassed housewife had suddenly to attend to one of the hundreds of domestic crises that occur in a normal household every day. It was all too nice, too prissy for Aveyard and the sergeant. Neither sat down, neither felt like it.

"Do you know this boy?" Aveyard asked, without preamble, showing the polaroid photograph to Fran. Fran looked at Malcolm Minton who, for once, was silent, his hand picking nervously at the sleeve of his quilted smoking jacket. "Yes," Fran said, "I know him." There was a silence, a clock ticking, boards squeaking, birds evensong silence. The clock chimed on the church tower, ten o'clock. They counted each stroke and waited.

"May I ask how you come to know the child?" Aveyard asked. Malcolm shook his head slightly, but the sergeant noticed. What's said is often less important than people's reactions; he'd trained himself, when two people were present at an interrogation, to watch reactions rather than listen to answers.

"I can't see that it's any of your business," Fran said. His voice was low, his manner not aggressive. It was a simple statement of fact; Aveyard couldn't quarrel with it. It *was* none of his business; there could be a million logical and legal explanations. Not that the law is logical, or that logic makes good law. "If I were to show you a picture of a boy called Martin, who lives in Bredgar . . .?"

"I'm afraid I'd still say it was none of your business." Again that quiet voice, insisting. If only I could get him angry, Aveyard thought; anger's an old policeman's weapon; people who become angry during an interrogation will often crack.

"Bristol? Liverpool?"

"Still none of your business, I'm afraid."

Dare he risk it? If he was wrong, he'd lose his witness. If he was right, perhaps Fran would crack. "But Norwich is my business, isn't it? Humphrey Holdeness would have something to say about Norwich, wouldn't he? Is that why Malcolm Minton killed him, on the bridge?"

Bingo, Malcolm quivered. Was it fear, rage, memory of hateful things said and done? "Holdeness knew you for what are you, a couple of old queers," the sergeant said. That did it. Malcolm Minton sprang to his feet, leaped forward as if he would assault the sergeant. Bruton stood his ground and what was about to become a blow became an ineffectual pat on the sergeant's rocklike chest. "You've no right to speak like that," Malcolm said, enraged. "You're just as bad as he was, as all the rest of them . . . Just because we're different. We've a right to live, haven't we? We don't do anyone any harm, do we? Answer me that, what harm do we do anybody? It's not like you men who go with women and get them pregnant, is it?" His voice rost to a shriek on the repugnant word pregnant.

"Why did you push Holdeness over the bridge?" the sergeant asked. "Was it because he called you a queer, just once too often. Did he torment you with it?"

"I didn't push him over the bridge."

"But you were there, you struck out at him just as you struck out at me, and because you're not man enough to hit anybody, you pushed him, just as you would have pushed me."

"I didn't push him over the bridge!"

"But you were *there*," Aveyard said, "we have a witness."

Malcolm Minton lifted his hands to his face. "He always was rude to Fran and me whenever he saw us. He'd never let us alone, jeering."

"And he jeered at you, on the bridge!" Aveyard said, driving hard.

Malcolm Minton nodded. "And you struck a blow at him, but it was only a tap . . ." Malcolm nodded again. "It was a tap," he said, "the merest tap. I don't believe in violence. I've never really hit anybody in my life, but I had to do something to stop him. I tapped him, on his chest. He pretended I'd hit him a severe blow. It was all pretending. He reeled about as if I'd really hit him, and he was tormenting me, calling Poweee, and Socko, and all those things from the cartoons, pretending I'd really hurt him, and then, as he was play-acting, he stumbled . . ."

"Against the parapet?"

"He stumbled and fell over. I went to the parapet, and looked over. I could see he was dead from the angle of his neck."

"And so you ran?" Aveyard said, his voice sympathetic.

"I'm afraid I did. I ran back here, well, not ran, just walked quickly." He looked up at Aveyard. "I'm not very brave," he said, "I never have been. Even at school, I was never very brave . . ." His voice tailed away. Aveyard looked at the sergeant who was perspiring, so intense had been his concentration. He shook his head. "Sit down, Mr Minton," the sergeant said, "you're not the only one. Very few of us are really brave when it comes to it, very few." Malcolm Minton sat down, looking straight in front of him. "I suppose you're going to charge us with perjury and all that," he said. "We lied to you about me being here."

"I'm not going to charge you with anything," Aveyard said. "There'll be an inquest on Holdeness next week, and you'll be called to give evidence since you were the last one to see him; if you tell the coroner exactly what you've told me, I'm quite certain he'll return a verdict of accidental death, and that's the last you'll ever hear of it."

"You believe me?" Malcolm Minton said, surprised.

"Yes, I do. After all, you wouldn't lie to my sergeant now. You've just said yourself, you're not very brave!" He smiled benevolently, old for his years. The sergeant nodded approvingly.

"Now, what about these children?" Aveyard asked, quietly.

Fran thought for a moment. "There's nothing illegal, you know?"

"I'm sure there isn't," Aveyard said, "but I'd like to get

the facts straight. Just for the record, you know."

"We both realised, a long time ago, that the only thing wrong with a life such as ours is that when you grow old, you have no-one to look after you. A married couple have children and grandchildren, but we have no-one, absolutely no-one. I shall go first," Fran said, "and then Malcolm will be left, all on his own."

"So you thought you'd create a ready-made family?"

"That's right."

"And you put them with foster parents so the children would get a good upbringing?"

"That's right. We knew it wouldn't be much of a life for a child, living with two old biddies like us!" He actually smiled; Malcolm smiled, too. All right, Aveyard thought, let 'em tell the story their own way.

"So you found a family with a good home, someone a bit older who wouldn't be having children of their own, and you got them to act as foster parents. You choose five places far apart, so that there was no likelihood the children would come together until you wanted them to, and you chose children at two-yearly intervals so they'd seem like natural brothers? And sisters?"

"Yes, brothers and sisters, just like a normal family."

"But where did you get the children in the first place?"

"From Grimsby. There's a Home for Unmarried Mothers. A friend of ours runs it, very kinky. Every two years I'd go up there, pay him a visit. He'd introduce me to all the girls over tea, I'd pick out one who seemed to be nice, take my chance, and have a little private chat to her. If she was agreeable, I'd take her out of the Home for Unmarried Mothers, put her in a private nursing home, and wait for her to have the baby."

"Then you'd resigter the birth on the short form that doesn't quote the father's name or the status of the mother, pay the girl a sum of money to disappear, and take the child over as your own. How much did you have to pay them?"

"It varied. You know what girls are. Some of them were avaricious. Martin's mother wouldn't take any money when she knew I'd bring the child up properly."

"But you never had yourself made legal guardian of any of these children?"

"I didn't need to!"

"The girls all signed a piece of paper naming you as the father!" the sergeant said. Fran nodded. "Obviously, you'd only pick girls who, for one reason or another, couldn't name the actual father. Either he was a married man or some such thing."

"That's right," Fran said.

"It was all legal," Malcom said, "and besides that, we were doing the children a good turn. What kind of upbringing could they expect as bastards. They'd either go to foster parents, chosen by the Government without the personal touch, or they'd have been dragged about by an unmarried mother! At least, we spared them that."

Aveyard shook his head, perplexed. No point of law sprang to mind and what Malcolm said was right, they had provided a good home for children who might otherwise not have got one, or been brought up in an Institution. Each of the children would have mother-love during its early years when it most needed it, and a stable family background.

"What are your future plans for the children?" Aveyard asked. "Shall you send them away to school?"

"We don't approve of boarding schools," Malcolm said, quickly.

Of course, they wouldn't! Is that where they'd both started. Many a boy is capable of normal sex, but is perverted by a too precious boarding school atmosphere. Many queers, of course, have never seen the inside of a boarding school, but there is a risk, however small.

"We've thought about this a lot," Fran said, "and decided we'll just let them make their own way in life until they're about eighteen. Then we'll see what we can do about helping financially, if they need it."

"You'll bring them here to live?"

"No, never . . . that would never do! No, we just want to have a family we can visit when we grow older. I've talked a lot about Malcolm, and they'll get to know him just as they know me. When I die he'll be a trustee of all the money. They'll get the money, you know, every bit of it . . ."

"Fran's been a good father to his children," Malcolm said, "and there's not many men can say that these days!"

When Bruton and Aveyard left the house, the sergeant was scratching his head. "Who's daft, Inspector," he asked, "us or them? 'Fran's been a good father to his children . . .'"

"You've never had a family?" Aveyard asked.

"No. It's been one of our regrets."

"You never thought of adoption?"

"Yes, we did at one time."

"But you never went through with it?"

They could see the police car waiting for them, at the bottom of the path that led to Tolly's. Late evening had not made the village any cooler; a hot June day turned into a hot June night. The sky was cloudless, scattered with an endless counting of stars so close they seemed to sparkle in the tops of the trees. Bruton sighed, and he was not the sort of man to sigh needlessly, or often. "I was young and foolish in those days," he said. "The adoption officer had a long talk with us, told us all about the duties and responsibilities of being a parent. When he'd gone I looked at my missis. 'Will you be very unhappy if we don't have one,' I asked her. After what he'd said, I just didn't think I qualified to be a father . . ."

They went silent down the lane to the waiting car. Aveyard had never known his own father, an articled solicitor's clerk who died early of bronchial pneumonia. His mother, a neat, clean, tidy soul had seen Aveyard through grammar school and into the police force, a safe job with a pension. Aveyard had been sent to University on a police training scheme, qualified with a BA (Social Science), became a detective. Promotion to sergeant and then inspector exceeded his mother's fondest hopes. When Aveyard was made inspector, the Chief had assigned Bruton to him more or less on permanent attachment. Neither emotion nor sentiment had any place between them; each maintained a correct relationship with the other that precluded intimacy, each could be official or informal as the occasion demanded. 'Not qualified', Aveyard thought, 'what balls!!'

"Where do you think we'll find Samantha Holdeness?" he said.

"In London, working as a waitress somewhere?"

"With three hundred and fifty pounds in her post office?"

"I expect so."

"And Christine? Two years old, no legs?"

"In Norwich. In a foster home, probably with a nurse for a mother, and an understanding father. She'll get all the love and attention she needs, and when she's old enough, she'll have a ready-made family of brothers and sisters, and enough money to cushion her through the hard times."

Both remembered Holdeness as they had seen him that morning in the police station. Was it only yesterday? "We've had a busy week-end," Aveyard said. They walked on towards the car.

"What about Mrs Gibbins?" the sergeant asked.

"Wartime love affair with one of the Free French who

was a bit too free? Had a baby. Kept it secret up there in the Hall. Baby dies, she knows the estate is entailed and can never be sold during her lifetime, so she gets her pal Nellie to give her a hand and they give the child a Christian burial. Holdeness has the parson's daughter in the bushes one day, sees her plant a flower over the grave, gets curious, goes to see why. Digs up a bone, is so scared he pushes the bone back in the soil and runs like bloody hell."

"Leaving the parson's daughter pregnant, looking for a glass of herbal tea!"

"Another old village custom?" Aveyard asked. "Let young Freeman get all excited about it tomorrow. Early turn for you and me; we'd better be getting home!"

Richard was in bed in Aveyard's spare room and Ingeborg was sitting on the sofa watching the ending of television. "Tea or coffee?" she asked, as she went into the kitchen.

"Coffee, white, no sugar!"

When she brought it to him the television had ended, and he had switched off. He was looking at the silent screen, thinking.

"I've been talking to Richard," she said, "he wants to go home first thing in the morning. He doesn't want his 'father' to know he ran away!"

"Where's home?"

"Newcastle, without a doubt. They've been very good to him; he's very fond of them."

"You ought to let *your* father know where you are!"

"I'll be going home later," she said as she sat beside him. He shook his head. "It isn't always like this," he said, "sometimes I don't have a case for weeks on end!"

"Ah, but the other times, days and nights away!"

"Working, all the time!"

"Oh, don't misunderstand me," she said, "I don't think

for a moment you'd be messing about with other women."

"Sergeant Bruton has a wife; she seems happy enough to have his slippers out."

"So would I be," Ingeborg said, "but I'd know that, when you were out we'd be two separate people, and I don't want that. Lots of men have wanted to marry me, but I could always see that it would be a question of two separate people. Me with my home life, looking for things to do to keep me happy, him with his work life, using me as the 'thing' to keep him happy! With you and I, it could be different."

He put his arm along her shoulder. "You feel that too, do you?" he asked, tenderly.

She nodded, blinking her eyes rapidly.

He drew her to him, held her, his hand tight on her shoulder. "I have to be a policeman," he said, "it's the only job I'm qualified for."

She forced a half-laugh. "That's rubbish," she said, "and you know it. You're one of those people who could do anything they set their minds to."

"So are you," he said persuasively.

"No, I'm not," she said. She sat upright, her moment of pain ended. "Your sergeant's wife is probably a very remarkable woman. And I'm not. No," she said, preventing him speaking, "I'm not fishing for compliments. I wouldn't mind at first, you having to stop whatever we were doing to dash out every time the telephone rings. But after a while, I know it'd start to bother me."

"I'd be on duty!"

"I know that. Being a policeman's wife, even being involved with a policeman except on a casual friendly basis—and that's something you and I could never do, we both know for us it's all or nothing!—well, being involved like that needs a very unselfish person, and that's probably where your sergeant's wife is stronger than I am."

The telephone rang.

"I just don't have the right qualifications," she said, as she handed him the instrument.

They'd found Christine with a nurse and her husband, in Norwich. Samantha was working in a coffee shop in the Earl's Court Road. When he put down the telephone, Ingeborg had already left.

"Damn," he said. The telephone rang again; he picked it up, savage.

"Of course, unless the Chief says otherwise, it's nothing to do with us," Jim Bruton said, "but I thought you'd like to know. Wilkins the horse-meat butcher has killed his three children and barricaded himself in his shop. Sam Gainer called 999 and we've got two squad cars there already. Wilkins has a shot-gun. And just one other little thing. Bent Hall's on fire and there's no sign of Mrs Gibbins. From the size of the blaze, it looks as if she's poured paraffin all over the place."

Aveyard put the telephone down.

It rang again, almost immediately.

"Yes, Chief," he said, "put my trousers back on and wait for the car . . ."